LETHAL SANGUINITY MEMOIRS OF A BLOOD WITCH

By Nefarious J.R. Bane

Content

PROLOGUE

Love—a word often twisted and misunderstood, reduced to a mere collection of emotions shared between two souls. Romance—a term crafted to sugarcoat the primal hunger of desire, to veil the raw need that pulses beneath the surface. Witch—a title cast like a curse, meant to damn even those who walk with the divine.

Yet here I stand, a soothsayer, a Tyliquin witch, born of the lust of a god and the willing submission of his creation. I am a paradox, revered by some as the last vestige of the old ways, despised by others as their ultimate damnation. I have served serpents whose hearts drip with corruption. I have been beaten, raped and sold into the frigid grip of slavery. Through every torment, from the agony of birth to the harsh trials of adulthood, one truth has remained unshakable: the love and unbreakable bond I share with my soul's keeper, a mythical beast of unfathomable power—King Calira Draconvieh.

As the threads of time wove their intricate patterns, many sought to uncover the secrets buried within my soul, to drag forth the skeletons locked away in the shadows of my past. Fate may have delayed my steps, tangled my path in its web, but now I stand before my destiny, clutching it with hands stained by blood and vengeance.

Within the pages of this ancient tome lies the story of my life—a tale of a mother, a lover, a warrior, and a teller of fortunes. But of all the chapters written, none hold greater weight than the story of Calira and I. It is a story of love so fierce, so true, that it was forged atop the bones of those who dared to keep us apart, and tempered in the blood of the women he took to his bed.

Some share their stories in hopes of garnering pity, while others believe their suffering demands the world's attention. But I am different. I reveal my secrets not for your sympathy, but to ignite your curiosity, to pull you into the depths of my existence. I want you to experience the raw reality of this world—its inhabitants, its shadows, and what it truly means to live as a witch.

To most, I am the embodiment of evil, a harbinger of damnation—a woman who would strike you down without hesitation, leaving you cold in your final breath. But what they fail to understand is that not all who wield the Sanguine Arts are born of sin. Some of us were forged into what we are by the very hands of those who now cower and point, blinded by their own ignorance and misunderstanding.

My name is Tonisa Tyliquin, and the book you now hold is not just a record of my past—it is a passage into the very depths of my mind.

ONE

Some would say my life began in the pure embrace of nature, untouched and untainted. Others believe I was cursed from the moment I drew my first breath, birthed from the womb of a mother whose face I'll never know. Yet, of this I am certain—whoever she was, she was a Tyliquin, just as I now stand. The brand upon my skin is proof enough.

I was born during the Embryonic Era, a time of great turmoil on Evernia, my home planet. It was an age when the humanoid inhabitants, in their arrogance, dared to take up arms against their betters. Dragons, hellhounds, wolves, witches, and sorcerers—each fighting for dominion over a world they believed was theirs to claim, though none had the true right.

For a time, the humans held the upper hand, their numbers and determination overwhelming the ancient powers. But their triumph was fleeting. The dragons, once scattered, united as one, driven by a purpose greater than themselves. At their helm was a force both feared and revered—a powerful Sanguine Witch known to all as the Abyssal Tyrant.

She tore away their shackles and set them free. Together, they claimed victory as a united force, standing strong against the tide of human ambition. But as I've said before, for every act of mercy, evil waits in the shadows, ready to strike. The fragile peace they had forged, the bond of allegiance that had once held them together, was shattered.

No longer bound by any restraint, the dragons turned on their savior. The northern serpents of La'Kum Manut Vey forged a kingdom atop the frozen corpses of those they turned to ice, their power as cold and unyielding as the landscape they ruled. Their southern kin, no less ruthless, consumed the very soil with rivers of fire, leaving the land barren and scorched—a testament to their wrath. Hellhounds were driven to the brink of extinction, their numbers dwindling to near nothingness, while the surviving humans were reduced to chains, enslaved by the very beings they once sought to conquer.

When the war finally came to its bitter end, a new horror swept across the land—a wave of genocide that sought to wipe the Tyliquin race from existence.

Magic became a crime punishable by death. In the dead of night, women and their children were dragged from their homes, torn from the safety of hearth and kin. Those fortunate—or unfortunate—enough to possess beauty found it their only currency, a meager bargaining chip in a world gone mad. They were sold into slavery, reduced to mere dolls, to be misused and paraded for the amusement of the dragons who now reveled in their newfound ability to assume a human form.

Nowhere was safe for our kind. The Tyliquin bloodline, rich with ancient power, was too potent to conceal. Our strength, once our greatest asset, had become a beacon that marked us for death or worse. The world had turned against us, and survival itself became a daily battle in a landscape where our very existence was deemed too dangerous to allow.

I was told by my adopted mother, Queen Raye'Zore, "You were born on a night of great calamity." She, the wife of King Ramsra Raye'Zore of Crystal Springs, had no hatchlings of her own when I came into their lives. It was for this reason, perhaps, that she granted me her mercy and pity. She often recounted the night I was left on their doorstep, swaddled in a thin, tattered cloth, the remnants of birth still clinging to my skin. She pulled me inside, washing away the ash that covered my tiny body, and when I was clean enough, she presented me to her husband. She claimed he agreed to let me stay, though in truth, it was more a curse than a blessing.

For as I grew older, I became what all Tyliquins were destined to be in the presence of such power and wealth—a slave.

My life was not one of a cherished child but of a servant, an ornament placed upon a pedestal to be admired for my oddity. The dragons, despite all we had done for them, took pleasure in our humiliation. We were nothing more than curiosities, our once-great power reduced to a source of their amusement. To be a Tyliquin in their world was to live a life of degradation, a life in which our dignity was stripped away as easily as the rags we wore.

The male dragons were notorious for seeking out young Tyliquin witches, corrupting their innocence and claiming dominance over them. It was a twisted game of power and ego, in which the capturers reveled in the control they held over these women.

You see, Tyliquin's were cursed with an unbreakable bond to the first man they lay with, forever bound to serve and love him. And so, a savage tradition began - the mass rape of girls as young as eleven. Once their maidenhood was taken, there was no escaping their fate. They became possessions of their rapists for eternity - condemned to a life of servitude and subservience. In those days, the thought of a slave trying to break free from their master was inconceivable. And for me, that is exactly what happened. My body violated, my spirit broken, and my trust shattered by those who claimed to protect me. The trifecta of rape, chains, and betrayal destroyed me from within, leaving me with nothing but a label - one that was forced upon me by others who could never understand the depths of my suffering.

I was a sweet girl once, full of foolish kindness and hopeless dreams. I was in love with a prince I knew I could never have—a dragon prince, the first heir to the most coveted throne on Evernia. I never imagined he would notice me, let alone see me for who I truly was. But one day, our eyes met, and it was as if they were forever bound, a connection that neither time nor fear could sever.

I was a pure magic wielder, forced to conceal my gifts, while he was the son of the king who held me in chains. I was nothing more than his father's slave, a figure shrouded in the rags of servitude. What could I possibly offer him but shame and the certainty of banishment or death? Yet, somehow, he overlooked the dark possibilities, seeing beyond the battered robes I was forced to wear. He saw me—the real me—and against all odds, we fell in love like fools, blind to the laws that forbade dragons and witches from ever becoming one.

Despite the ever-present threat of being torn from the waking world, Calira and I forged a bond that would last a lifetime. We may have been reckless in our love, but we were not without caution. We hid our romance in the shadows, shrouded in fear of his father's wrath and the ever-watchful eyes of the public. The risks were immense, but in each other, we found a refuge, a place where the impossible became our reality. We loved in secret, knowing that if we were discovered, it would mean the end of everything we held dear. But in those stolen moments, we were free—free to dream, free to love, and free to hope that somehow, against all odds, we could defy the world and make our love endure.

We met in secret, once every fortnight, slipping away from the ever-watchful eyes of the guards. In those hidden moments,

he could have taken me by force, as so many others had done to those like me. He could have claimed me as his own, raped me if I had resisted, or beaten me into submission. But he never did. Instead, he showed me a kindness and compassion I had never known.

His touch was gentle, his hands warm and steady, yet he never asked to share my bed. He stole the sweetest of baked treats and had them delivered to my chamber in the dead of night, each morsel a silent promise of his affection. During the day, he would find excuses to pass by me, taking on tasks that led him in my direction, just to catch a glimpse of me, to gift me with a smile that could brighten even my darkest hours.

Some noticed his infatuation, whispering rumors and casting suspicious glances. Others assumed his kindness came with strings attached, that there was a debt I would eventually be forced to repay in the most devious of ways. I braced myself for that day, expecting the inevitable demand, the cruel twist that would turn his tenderness into a weapon against me.

But that day never came—not from him. With Calira, there were no hidden agendas, no cruel expectations. He gave freely, not seeking to take anything from me in return. In him, I found a love that was pure, a love that defied the harsh reality of the world we lived in. And in those stolen moments, I allowed myself to believe, if only for a little while, that we could find a way to be together, despite all that stood against us.

Despite all our caution, someone eventually saw us. We had stolen a kiss beneath the silver rays of the moon, a moment of passion and tenderness that we thought was ours alone. But the shadows have eyes, and that night, those eyes belonged to someone with the power to unravel everything we had so carefully concealed.

I always suspected it was Lady Eiwa, the jealous wretch who trailed after Calira with a desperation that bordered on madness. She had long coveted him, clinging to the belief that she was meant to be his betrothed, despite the fact that he never spared her more than a passing glance. In her mind, she was already his, and my presence was an insult she could not tolerate.

That night, as we tore ourselves away from each other, hearts pounding with the thrill of stolen affection, we were blissfully unaware of the storm brewing just out of sight. The rain of turmoil that would soon drench us in despair was already gathering, and we had unknowingly set it in motion with that single, forbidden kiss.

I remember folding into my bed that night, curling around my pillow, inhaling the lingering scent of him. My heart still races from our stolen kiss, my lips tingling with the memory. I closed my eyes, letting myself sink into the warmth of that moment, when suddenly, the door to my chamber was kicked open. I barely had time to gasp before rough hands seized me. I screamed, but the sound was cut short by a brutal gauntlet to my cheek.

Pain exploded across my face, and I was yanked from my bed, my hair twisted cruelly in the knight's grip as he drug me down the cold, unforgiving stone corridor of the keep. I could feel the rough surface tearing at my skin, the sharp sting of blood trickling down my legs. Every jolt, every scrape, sent waves of agony through me, but I was too stunned to do anything but endure it.

When he finally released me, I collapsed to the floor, my body throbbing with pain. I lifted my head, and through the haze of tears, I saw King Ramsra Raye'Zore towering over Calira, lecturing him with a voice like thunder. Calira stood before him, six inches shorter, his black hair bowed low, his arms folded behind his back in a posture of submission. He looked so small, so defeated under the towering presence of his father, whose arctic white hair seemed to blaze with the fury of his words.

As I struggled to focus, their attention shifted to me. The knight who dragged me there took his leave, sealing the door behind him with a finality that echoed in the silence that followed. The air was thick with tension, and I knew that whatever came next would change everything.

Ramsra strode toward me, and before I could even think to plead for forgiveness, his hand lashed out. The force of the blow sent me sprawling to the floor. I hit the cold stone hard, the impact jarring through my body. The pain was sharp, but the humiliation was sharper. I laid there at his feet, trembling, every breath a struggle, a stark reminder of my helplessness.

Calira stood silent, offering no words in my defense. His fear of his father was well known. I could see it in the way he trembled, his gaze locked on the ground, as if avoiding the monster's eyes might somehow protect him. The creature before us, a towering figure of rage and cruelty, glared down with a hatred that ran deep, a hatred that had festered since the day Calira hatched. His scales, dark as the abyss, had always marked him as different, cursed in the eyes of his father, who desired only the gleam of platinum—a color that was never meant to be.

I was commanded never to look upon the prince again, under the penalty of death. The weight of our unspoken longing was undeniable, but no desire could justify the sacrifice of our lives. When I was finally dismissed, I limped back to my chamber, only to find it stripped of all warmth and familiarity. Every token of Calira's kindness, every treasure born of our secret adoration, had vanished.

Desperation seized me as I rushed to the window, only to witness the cruel spectacle below. My cherished belongings, symbols of our forbidden love, were being consumed by flames in the courtyard. Tears, bitter and relentless, streamed down my face as I watched my past reduced to ashes. With a heart full of anguish, I tore myself from the window and collapsed onto my bed.

I called upon the gods with fervent pleas, begging them to pave a path for our reunion, to bless our forbidden union. Morning after morning, night after night, I offered prayers and sacrifices, but it seemed my words were lost in the void, unheard and unheeded. Yet, in my despair, I failed to realize that the gods had indeed listened.

In my naïveté, I expected instant mercy, but the cosmos does not grant favors lightly. I had already been bestowed with much; now, it was time for fate and the dark shrines of corrupt nature to exact their price.

TWO

Four moons had waxed and waned since that fateful night when we were discovered in each other's arms, our secret exposed under the pale light of the stars. I had since returned to my life of service, slipping back into the shadows where I belonged. My days were filled with quiet submission, my voice a mere whisper on the wind, my gaze fixed on the ground.

That morning, I was summoned to bring the breaking meal to the king and queen. With a tray balanced in my trembling hands, I ascended the spiraling staircase that led to their private chambers. The air grew thick with tension as I approached, the echo of harsh words reverberating down the stone walls, drowning out the soft jingle of the coins at my ankles.

As I reached the top, the door stood slightly ajar, and through the narrow gap, I could see the king towering over his queen. His voice was a tempest, each word a thunderclap, and then it came—

the venomous accusation that froze my blood. "Adulterous whore," he spat, the words slithering from his lips like a curse.

My breath caught in my throat, and I stumbled back, the tray slipping from my fingers. The teacup shattered on the ground, its delicate pieces scattering like lost hopes. In that moment of silence, I heard it—the sickening sound of steel slicing through flesh, a noise that would haunt me for the rest of my days.

Tears blurred my vision as I turned to flee, but before I could take a step, a hand clamped down on my arm, iron-strong and unyielding. The king yanked me into the room, the force of his grip leaving bruises in its wake. The door slammed shut behind me, the bolt sliding into place with a finality that stole the breath from my lungs. There would be no escape.

There I stood, trembling, a chill creeping through my bones despite the warmth of the room. The fear gnawed at my insides, a relentless beast whispering that I might never see the light of day again. The king moved behind me, his presence a dark cloud that swallowed all hope. His hands, cold and claw-like, dug into my cheeks, forcing my gaze upon the scene of horror before me.

His marital bed, once a symbol of royal elegance, was now a blood-soaked altar of despair. The queen lay sprawled across it, her body marred by the savage wounds that gaped in her chest and throat. Blood pooled beneath her, staining the silken sheets a deep, unforgiving crimson. I could still hear the brittle, rasping sound that escaped her lips as she fought for breath, a sound so fragile it seemed the very air might shatter it.

He made me watch as the life drained from her eyes, the flicker of consciousness fading into the void of death. One moment, she was there, clinging desperately to the world, and the next, she was gone—a shell, an echo of the woman she had been.

A profound sadness welled up within me, mingling with the terror, as I thought of the time it took to nurture life, to bring it into this world, only for it to be snuffed out in the blink of an eye.

Ramsra's grip tightened around my neck, his fingers cold and unyielding as iron. With a vicious shove, he forced me toward the bed, his breath hot and foul against my ear as he hissed his vile threats. He spoke of the fate of all whores, how they met their end in ways just as cruel, and how I would be no different if I dared to defy him. His words were a dark promise, one that chilled me to the core.

With a sudden, brutal force, he thrust me headfirst into the thick pool of blood that soaked the sheets. The queen's lifeblood clung to me, its warmth already fading, its smell overwhelming. I couldn't breathe—my lungs screamed for air, but the thick, metallic taste of blood filled my mouth, choking any sound I tried to make. My screams died on my lips, swallowed by the crimson tide. Panic surged through me, and I struggled to lift my head, but his weight pinned me down, unrelenting.

As I fought for breath, I felt the thin silks of my robes yanked violently over my back, leaving me exposed and vulnerable. My terror turned to dread as I realized what was to come, and I thrashed beneath him, desperate to escape. But Raye'Zore, with all his twisted strength, held me down as if I were nothing more than a rag doll.

What followed was a brutality I could never have imagined. The pain tore through me, a searing, relentless agony as he violated me, each thrust like fire through my body. My mind screamed in protest, but there was no escape, no refuge from the horror. I had been untouched, pure even in the harsh life I had lived, and now that innocence was ripped from me with merciless cruelty.

The room spun, the edges of my vision darkening as the pain threatened to consume me. But in that moment of despair, I managed to turn my head, gasping for air. The blood-soaked sheets beneath me were a constant reminder of the life that had been taken, and now, the life that was being shattered. And yet, even as I stole that breath, I knew there would be no reprieve, only the unending nightmare of his violence.

His claws raked across my back, each vicious swipe etching deep, jagged scars into my flesh—marks that would remain long after the physical pain had faded. I fought to disconnect from the horror, to retreat into the safe corners of my mind, where memories of Calira's kindness might offer some comfort. But no matter how hard I tried, the darkness swallowed me whole, pulling me down into the abyss where there was no escape, no sanctuary.

The curse of my race, the one whispered about in shadowed corners, began to stir within me. It was a dark, ancient thing, a power that slumbered until pain and suffering woke it. I felt it rising, like a serpent coiling in my soul, feeding on the torment that Ramsra inflicted upon me. But even as the curse threatened to consume me, to transform me into something other than myself, there was one thing that burned itself into my memory— one thing that would haunt me long after this nightmarish ordeal.

It was something Ramsra said, a cruel whisper as he tore my innocence away forever. His voice, dripping with malice, slithered into my ear, poisoning my mind as his body defiled mine. The words cut deeper than his claws, branding themselves onto my soul.

"You wanted to be the lover of a prince, and now you have the king. You will forever be mine."

Those words, dripping with venom, continue to haunt my nights, turning even the smallest hope of peace into a storm of nightmares. Ramsra's cruel proclamation has bound itself to my soul, a dark promise that lingers in the corners of my mind, twisting my dreams into grotesque reflections of that night.

When he was finally done with me, he pulled away, leaving me broken and bleeding on the blood-soaked bed. Without a word, he strode from the room, his steps echoing in the silence that followed, as if the very air had been stripped of life. I lay there for what felt like an eternity, too shattered to move, the weight of what had happened pressing down on me like a suffocating blanket.

But eventually, I forced myself to rise. With trembling hands, I gathered the tattered remnants of my robes and stumbled toward the hidden passageway I had once used to slip in and out of the castle unnoticed. It led me back to my humble chamber, where I collapsed, broken and alone.

Two days passed in a blur of pain and despair. I neither ate nor drank, too lost in the darkness that had swallowed my spirit. I prayed for the end to come, for some merciful force to release me from the torment of my memories. But no such release came. Instead, a harsh knock shattered the fragile silence of my solitude.

They came for me then, dragging me from my chamber and into the harsh light of day. My body ached with every step, the wounds both seen and unseen fresh and raw. I was taken before the king and his court, their eyes cold and judgmental, as if they already knew the outcome of this twisted trial. The news of Queen Raye'Zore's death had spread through the kingdom, and the finger of blame pointed squarely at me.

I stood there, trembling, as the accusations were laid out. I was convicted of the murder of Queen Raye'Zore, the crime for which I would now pay a price. But instead of the swift embrace of death that I might have welcomed, I was met with something else—banishment. The king, the very man who had stolen my innocence and shattered my life, decreed this sentence.

With twisted logic, he declared that because of his wife's alleged adulterous behavior, my actions were somehow justified, but still, a crime. It was a cruel irony, a punishment designed not to end my suffering, but to prolong it. Banishment, he said, was mercy—his mercy. But I knew the truth. This was his way of keeping me within his grasp, ensuring that no matter where I went, I would always be haunted by the memory of what he had done to me.

And so, I was cast out, not just from the castle, but from the life I had known, into a world that would see me as nothing more than a murderer and a whore. The king's words, like chains, bound me to a fate I could not escape, a future as dark as the nightmares that plagued my sleep.

Calira was there, standing among the court, but he would not meet my eyes. The man who had once shown me kindness, whose touch had been gentle, now looked upon me with a scowl of disbelief and pain. His face, twisted in anguish, was a mirror of my own shattered heart. It was as if the bond we had shared had been severed by the cruel blade of fate, leaving behind only bitterness and sorrow.

The men around him were pitiless. With rough hands, they stripped me of my clothing, exposing my fresh wounds and my vulnerable body to the eyes of the court. Shame burned through me as I stood there, naked and trembling, each bruise and scar a testament to the horrors I had endured. My dignity, like my innocence, was taken from me in that moment, leaving me feeling more like a broken doll than a person.

Without a word, they dragged me through the castle, my bare feet scraping against the harsh ground. The world around me blurred, the faces of the court fading into a sea of judgmental stares. Then, with a final, brutal shove, they cast me out beyond the castle walls, the iron gate slamming shut behind me with a deafening finality.

I was only nineteen—barely more than a child—and yet I was expected to survive in a world that had shown me nothing but cruelty. I had no supplies, not even a scrap of clothing to protect me from the elements, and certainly no weapon to defend myself against the dangers that lurked in the wild. They had thrown me to the wolves, a lamb without a shepherd, and expected me to fend for myself.

So, I walked. I walked until the looming shadows of the forest swallowed me whole, the dense canopy overhead blotting out the light. Each step was a struggle, my body weakened by pain and exhaustion, but I pressed on, driven by the last remnants of my will to survive.

In the silence of the forest, where the only sounds were the rustling of leaves and the distant calls of creatures unseen, I found the one strength they could not strip from me—my magic. It pulsed within me, a force as ancient as the soil itself, waiting to be unleashed. It was the only thing that kept me moving forward, the only weapon I had left.

THREE

There I was, a shadow among shadows, running frantically through the forest under the shroud of night. The darkness wrapped around me like a cloak, and though nothing tangible pursued me, the primal fear that gnawed at my heart told a different story. It's a curious thing, the mind of a hunted creature—whether by beast or by memory, it can conjure terrors out of mere whispers. Every rustle of leaves, every creak of wood sent my pulse racing, as if some unseen force wished to see me dead. The fine hairs on my body stood on end, gooseflesh prickling my skin as if warning me of dangers lurking just beyond the edge of sight.

Banished during the first song of winter, the cold clung to the air but had yet to show its true teeth. Still, it was enough to pierce through the thin layer of warmth I had left, chilling me to the bone. The forest around me seemed to speak in a tongue I had never known, an ancient, cryptic language woven from the sigh of the wind through the branches and the murmur of the leaves beneath my feet. A place that had once offered me solace, where I had often wandered to escape my thoughts, now felt like an arena of unknown dangers, each shadow a potential threat.

Twigs snapped underfoot, their brittle bones cracking beneath the weight of my desperation. The forest floor was a minefield of thorns and sharp stones, and each step left a mark.

Even now, I carry the scars from that night, reminders of the fear and pain that drove me forward. The wind was my only companion, howling through the trees, its icy fingers tearing at my face, and the broken branches left stinging welts as they lashed across my skin.

The wind began to pick up, a restless spirit that urged me onward. I knew my options were limited: a three-day journey to Arobren City, where the stone walls might offer protection but little else, or a shorter trek to the Village of Naon. I chose the latter, driven by the hope that the people of Naon would take pity on me. The natives there were known for their kindness, their open hearts, and their willingness to help those in need. They, like me, had magic in their veins, a bond that I prayed would stir their compassion.

Naon was a place where the old ways still held sway, where the people lived in harmony with the forest and its secrets. If I could reach them, I knew they would not turn me away. Perhaps they would provide me with clothing to guard against the cold, a bit of food, and some meager supplies—just enough to see me through to Arobren.

And so, I ran, driven by the flickering hope that somewhere ahead lay a chance for survival, for sanctuary. The forest loomed around me, dark and unyielding, but in my heart, I held onto the belief that the people of Naon would not let one of their own perish in the wilderness. That belief was all that kept me moving, each step a painful reminder of the price I had paid, and the uncertain future that awaited me.

I had walked for what felt like an eternity, the relentless march of time measured only by the agony in my legs and the deepening wounds on the soles of my feet. Each step sent a jolt of pain up my legs, my muscles burning with exhaustion. The chill of the forest clung to me, my body filthy and aching, and the hunger gnawing at my stomach was a dull but constant reminder of my frailty. I was a wraith, a shadow of the person I had once been, but I pressed on, driven by the desperate need to find shelter.

As the day bled into twilight, my weary eyes caught sight of something hidden among the dense trees—a small, abandoned cottage, half-swallowed by the forest. It was a crumbling relic of a time long past, its roof sagging under the weight of years, the wood rotting and darkened by the elements. But to me, it was a sanctuary, a place where I could escape the biting cold and the haunting memories that trailed me.

From what little I knew, this cottage had once belonged to an exile, a soul cast out from society much like myself. It seemed fitting then, that I should find refuge here, in a place forgotten by the world. With a mix of trepidation and hope, I approached the door, pushing it open with trembling hands.

Inside, the air was thick with the smell of damp wood and decay, but it was warm, and more importantly, it was safe. The interior was sparse, the furnishings long since worn down by neglect, but there, amid the dust and cobwebs, I found a treasure—piles of dirty clothing, left behind by whoever had once called this place home. The fabric was old and rough, stained with the passage of time, but I had never been so grateful to see linen in my entire life.

Back at the Crystaline Keep, washing bedding and linens had been the chore I loathed most, the endless scrubbing and rinsing a monotonous task that left my hands raw and aching. But now, those memories felt distant, almost foreign, as I clutched the dirty garments to my chest, feeling a strange sense of joy wash over me. These rags, unwanted and forgotten, were more precious to me now than the finest silks.

I hurried inside, closing the door behind me as if to shut out the world beyond. There was little in the way of comfort—an old, creaking chair, a table with one leg shorter than the others, and a fireplace long cold and barren. But for a girl who had nothing, this meager offering was a bounty. It was a place to rest, to gather my strength, and perhaps, to begin anew.

In that tiny, decrepit cottage, I found a sliver of hope. It wasn't much, but it was enough. Enough to keep me moving forward, enough to remind me that even in the darkest of times, there is something to cling to, no matter how small.

I sifted through the pile of clothing, my fingers brushing against fabric that had long since begun to succumb to the relentless passage of time. Most of it was brittle with dry rot, the threads unraveling at the slightest touch. Still, I continued my search, hoping to find something, anything, that could serve as more than a rag. After what felt like hours, I came across a single blouse, its fabric worn but intact. The material was surprisingly fine, a delicate weave that suggested whoever had lived here had once known the touch of luxury—perhaps a lover from a life far removed from this desolate place.

I slipped the blouse over my head, the fabric cool against my skin. It hung loosely on my small frame, the hem brushing just past the swell of my thighs. It wasn't much, but it was something, and in that moment, it felt like a shield against the harshness of the world outside.

With the blouse clinging to me like a second skin, I ventured back into the night, the darkness pressing in from all sides. I found a small bowl among the meager possessions left behind, and I took it with me, intending to gather what I could to sustain myself. It was a slow, laborious process, the gathering of water from a nearby stream, collecting enough wood and leaves to start a small fire. The forest around me seemed indifferent to my struggle, its ancient trees whispering secrets I could not understand as I worked.

By the time I had what I needed, hours had passed, and my body ached with the effort. But I managed to build a small fire within the fireplace of the cottage, its flames flickering weakly in the darkness. The heat was a welcome relief, a fragile warmth that seeped into my bones as I set about washing the few items I had found. The water was cold, and the fabric resisted the dirt that had set in over years of neglect, but I scrubbed with determination, as if by doing so I could cleanse more than just the stains—perhaps a part of my own suffering as well.

As I worked, my stomach churned with hunger, the gnawing ache in my belly intensifying with every passing moment. The growls had turned into sharp waves of pain, and my head throbbed with the realization of just how dire my situation had become. I regretted every meal I had taken for granted back at the Crystaline Keep, where food had been plentiful if not always to my liking. Here, in the heart of the forest, the prospect of filling my stomach seemed a distant hope.

Desperation drove me to search beyond the cottage, and I soon stumbled upon a cluster of berry bushes not far from where I would spend the night. The berries were small and bitter, their taste more medicinal than nourishing, but I had no choice. I ate them slowly, each sour bite barely easing the gnawing pain in my stomach. They did little to satisfy my hunger, but they kept me from the brink of collapse, and that was all I could ask for.

Returning to the cottage, I settled near the fire, my body wrapped in the oversized blouse, my thoughts a jumble of fear and exhaustion. The night stretched on, endless and unforgiving, but within the confines of that small house, I found a sliver of safety. It was enough to see me through the night, enough to keep the darkness at bay, if only for a little while.

I lay sprawled on the unforgiving stone, offering a silent prayer to the gods. Though my body ached with the chill that seeped into my bones, I found solace in the fact that, at least here, I was sheltered from the harsh elements that raged beyond the walls. The tendrils of sleep began to weave their way through my mind, pulling me back to a time when I was safe and warm, cradled in the embrace of my dragon—my one true love, whom I had resigned myself to never see again.

As the veil of dreams descended, my thoughts turned to him. What was he doing now? Did he ever think of me since I was torn from the sanctuary of his home? My heart ached with longing; I missed him with every fiber of my being. The memory of his lips against mine, the way his presence made me feel whole—these were the things I yearned for most. Yet, such tender thoughts curdled into bitter poison within me. I was no longer the woman I once was. I had become damaged, tainted by the cruel will of his father—or so I believed.

I cannot say how long I drifted in that twilight between sleep and waking, but when my eyes finally fluttered open, the moonlight still spilled through the narrow window. I was jolted from my slumber by the searing touch of a familiar presence. A sharp, burning pain followed as a claw traced the line of my eyelid, forcing it open. I screamed, panic and confusion flooding my senses as I struggled to comprehend who stood before me. My mind raced, disbelief battling with hope, for I had never expected to see him again. His father had made sure of that.

I sat up, shock rendering me mute, as fear clawed at my heart. I trembled, not for myself alone, but for him. If we were discovered together, the consequences would be fatal for us both.

Calira was as intoxicating as ever, a potent blend of raw power and rugged grace. His beard was thick and meticulously groomed, framing a face both fierce and beautiful, while his unruly hair cascaded down his back, a wild contrast to the fire that blazed within his eyes. Beneath the gleaming armor that hugged his form, his body had begun to harden with the transition from youth to manhood, every movement a testament to the strength he had earned. He came to me bearing gifts—food, water, and a few simple garments. But more than that, he brought warmth in the form of blankets and, to my astonishment, a horse.

That night, our passions ignited with an intensity that seemed to scorch the very air around us. We came together with a fervor that made me tremble with the fear that my cries of pleasure would betray us, until his own roars of ecstasy filled the night, drowning out all else. Our lovemaking was relentless, a fevered dance that lasted hours, each moment more consuming than the last, until at last, he spilled his seed deep within me. I collapsed beside him, our bodies entwined, slick with sweat and the remnants of our fierce coupling.

For the first time, I tasted the true pleasure that can exist between a man and a woman—pleasure that was mine by choice, a reclamation of the power that had been stolen from me. The specter of Ramsra, though his wounds still marred my flesh, faded into the background, a shadow eclipsed by the blazing light of my newfound freedom. That night, I banished the memory of his violation, erasing it with the tender yet primal act of love I shared with the beast I adored.

Calira, with concern etched upon his brow, asked why I had not bled for him. I lied—swiftly, seamlessly—telling him that I had been defiled by a passing guard on my journey from Crystal Springs. The grim reality of such tales in our land made my words believable, and he accepted them without question. Though I despised his father, I could not bear to turn Calira against him— not for my sake. Ramsra was all he had left in this world, and I would not be the one to tear that bond asunder.

As swiftly as he had come, he left me, leaving behind only his gifts and the remnants of his passion that now trickled between my thighs. I watched him mount his horse—a magnificent black stallion with a mane that swept the ground like a curtain of midnight. True to his nature, the prince couldn't resist a final display of prowess. With a flourish, he guided his steed into a tight circle, his lips pursed in a teasing kiss aimed in my direction. The stallion reared, its powerful whinny slicing through the night, a testament to the bond it shared with its master.

I stood in the doorway, helpless but to watch as he galloped away, swallowed by the darkness. He was strength incarnate, a force of nature that could not be contained. And yet, despite the chasm of fate and circumstance that yawned between us, he was mine. No matter what misfortunes sought to tear us apart, our bond was unbreakable.

For a moment, I leaned against the doorframe, my heart heavy with the weight of his departure. Then, as if compelled by a force beyond my control, I stepped forward, my feet moving of their own accord. The pain that had once throbbed in my soles was now a distant memory, replaced by a sharper, more agonizing ache in my chest. I wept as I ran after him, my cries lost to the wind as he vanished into the night. He never looked back. Onward he rode, until the darkness claimed him entirely, leaving me alone in the cold silence.

And then, it struck me with the force of a revelation. I was not merely a Tyliquin—I was something more, something greater. Despite the torment I had endured, my heart still burned with love and desire for Calira, while all I felt for my attacker was a seething hatred and an insatiable thirst for vengeance. This epiphany, as painful as it was, filled me with a strange sense of hope. It gave me the strength to sleep that night, knowing that our paths would cross again.

For in my heart, I knew that Calira and I were destined for one another. The gods themselves had woven our fates together, and not even the cruel whims of the universe could keep us apart.

FOUR

In the days that followed my fateful union with Prince Raye'Zore, life seemed to drain of its prior excitement. The thrill of that primal bond faded into the mundane, leaving me to endure a monotonous journey that stretched on like an eternity. Days blended into nights as I rode through the unforgiving wilderness, the solitude pressing down upon me with each passing hour. I had never ventured so far on my own, and the unfamiliarity of the land soon turned treacherous. I found myself lost, wandering along the wrong paths, my horse's strength ebbing with every weary step.

Though I paused each day to let her graze, the desolate roads offered little respite. The world seemed to shrink around us, barren and empty, until at last, I crested the hill that overlooked the sprawling city of Arobren. Exhaustion clung to me like a second skin; every muscle ached, and my spirit sagged under the weight of the journey. The provisions that Calira had so generously bestowed upon me were long gone, devoured by the unrelenting march of time.

But despite my weariness, I knew that survival demanded more of me. With a heavy heart, I urged my mare onward, and together we descended into Arobren, both of us wary of the unknown. The city teemed with life, its streets alive with the hustle and bustle of men, women, and children, all immersed in the rhythm of their daily lives. Yet amidst the throngs, I felt the pull of the unknown, the whisper of fate beckoning me deeper into the heart of this unfamiliar world.

I dismounted, guiding my weary companion—my only friend—through the labyrinth of bustling streets. The rhythmic clatter of her hooves against the cobblestone still echoes in my mind, a steady beat that anchored me amidst the chaos of the city. The tantalizing aroma of freshly baked bread wafted through the air, tugging at my empty stomach with a hunger that bordered on desperation. I've always had a deep appreciation for good food, and in that moment, the scent alone was enough to make me forget my troubles, if only for a fleeting second.

But the reality of my situation quickly set in. The common folk paid me little heed as I wandered through the city, my presence barely registering in their busy lives. I moved from door to door, humbling myself before strangers, offering my hands for whatever work they might have, no matter how menial. I was prepared to trade sweat and toil for a single meal, a modest exchange that became the rhythm of my days for weeks on end.

Some days, fortune smiled upon me, and I found work that filled my belly. But on others, I went hungry, left to endure the gnawing emptiness inside. As the days bled together, the relentless grip of poverty tightened around me. Eventually, I was forced to make a heart-wrenching decision. My mare, once my steadfast companion, had grown gaunt and frail, much like myself. She deserved more than I could give, and so, with a heavy heart, I traded her to a farmer just beyond the city gates for a few silver coins.

It was a bitter farewell. I hated to part with her, but I knew she would fare better under the care of someone who could provide the stable life I could not. Watching her fade into the distance, I felt the cold bite of loneliness anew, but I took solace in knowing she would no longer starve or shiver in the night.

I managed to scrape by, finding work here and there with those who didn't shy away from the sight of a marked witch in their midst. My tasks were as varied as they were humble—I cooked in the dim, smoky kitchens of taverns, scrubbed the grand garderobes of the wealthy, and even served as the market maid for a prominent family. Each job, no matter how small or degrading, was a means to survive, a way to keep my belly full and my mind occupied.

Then came the day that changed everything. I was at the market, dutifully collecting the items from the list I'd been given, when a woman approached me. She was no ordinary woman; even from a distance, it was clear she commanded a certain respect, though not in the way one might expect. I recognized her—a harlot, and a well-known one at that. I'd seen her before, often in the shadows, once even in the throes of a carnal act with a man in a dark alley.

But today, she was different. She wore fine linens, richly colored and expertly tailored, garments that marked her as someone of considerable influence. Her lips curled into a smirk, a look that spoke of confidence and power as men trailed after her, bewitched by her presence like dogs chasing a scent. There was something in her gaze as she approached me—something knowing, as if she saw past the surface, past the mark on my skin, and into the very depths of who I was.

In that moment, I sensed that our meeting was no mere chance encounter. There was an unspoken understanding between us, a connection that transcended the mundane. As she closed the distance between us, I felt the weight of destiny shift, a new path unfurling before me, one that would lead far beyond the market stalls and menial labor that had defined my life thus far.

I was elbow-deep in a barrel of apples, carefully selecting the ripest ones, when I felt a tap on my shoulder. Instinct took over before reason had a chance to catch up. I spun on my heel, my fingers already curling around the hilt of a dagger—a gift from Sir Wanson, my keeper and protector. He had warned me countless times of the dangers lurking in the city, especially for someone like me—a Tyliquin, feared and misunderstood. The dagger was to be my first and last line of defense, only to be drawn when absolutely necessary. In the hands of a Tyliquin, even a simple blade carried the weight of dark possibilities, for none truly knew how deeply our roots intertwined with the Sanguine Arts.

So, when I turned to face the woman, dropping the apple I'd been holding and pressing the blade to her throat in one swift motion, her sharp intake of breath echoed between us. Her hands shot up in surrender, and she took a step back, her eyes wide but not with fear—more with surprise. She was striking, even in that moment of tension, with long blonde hair that gleamed under the daylight. Her eyes were a vivid green, almost unnaturally so, and she towered over most women with a stature that commanded attention—six foot six, and built like a goddess sculpted by a master's hand. There was an air about her, a rare creation with an attitude to match.

"Easy there, girl," she murmured, her voice low and soothing, yet laced with amusement. "I'm not here to harm you."

My hand trembled as I lowered the knife, heart pounding in my chest. I prayed silently that no one had witnessed my reckless act, for in this city, a witch—even one defending herself—was always seen as the villain. Our mere existence was a crime, a sin etched into our skin by the fear of others, and the punishment was death without mercy.

My mind flashed back to a lesson taught to me long ago, by my adopted mother, before the cruel hand of fate had claimed her life. I had been only five years old when she first spoke the words that would shape my future, words that echoed now in my mind as I stood trembling before the woman who had so easily provoked my fear. The lesson was simple, but its truth profound, a reminder that the world would never see us for what we truly were—only for what they feared we might become.

"There are only three kinds of power a woman will ever hold in this man's world," my mother had told me, her voice heavy with the weight of experience. "Her beauty, her silence, and the cunt that rests between her thighs. Lose any of the three, and you'll find yourself stripped of worth in their eyes."

These were the words that had been etched into my soul from a tender age, a grim truth passed down from a being who had seen too much of the world's cruelty. Beauty, silence, and flesh—these were the currencies by which women were measured, valued, and discarded. In a world governed by the patriarchy, these were the tools a woman could wield to carve out her place, or the chains that bound her to a life of subjugation.

I understood this lesson all too well as I stood there, trembling, the dagger now sheathed but my heart still racing. The woman before me embodied all three—her beauty undeniable, her silence kept until the perfect moment, and her body a weapon that commanded respect, or at the very least, a twisted form of reverence.

In that moment, I realized that the power my mother had spoken of wasn't just a means of survival—it was a double-edged sword. A woman could wield it to control her fate, but just as easily, it could be used against her, stripping away her worth in the eyes of those who saw only what they desired. And as I gazed into the green eyes of the woman before me, I knew that she, too, understood this dark wisdom, perhaps better than anyone I had ever met.

My stepmother had been right—those words of hers echoed in my mind every single day. Her wisdom, though profound, had not been enough to save her in the end. She had fallen, not by the cruelty of strangers, but by the very hands of the beast who had sworn an oath to protect her. The bitter irony of it still gnawed at me, a reminder that trust was a fragile thing, easily shattered and leaving nothing but ruins in its wake.

From that day forward, I vowed never to be a victim again. It mattered not if the threat came from a man of mere flesh or a creature clad in the scales of a dragon—I would be my own guardian, my own shield against the world's dangers. I would never again allow myself to be at the mercy of another's whims or betrayals.

I studied the woman before me, taking in every detail, every nuance of her posture and expression. She was a mystery wrapped in fine linens, her confident demeanor a stark contrast to the submissive role her profession might suggest. There was power in her, and it intrigued me, though I was not foolish enough to trust it blindly.

"What name do you go by?" I asked, my voice steady despite the turmoil that still churned within me. The question was simple, but its answer could reveal much about the woman who stood before me—whether she was friend or foe, ally or adversary, or something far more complicated.

"They call me Consivayae," she replied, her lips curving into a smile that held the secrets of countless men. Her voice carried a confidence born of experience, and she began to tell me of the freedom she had found in the life she led as a whore. It was a freedom I had never considered, one that came not from the absence of chains, but from the power to choose how those chains were worn. If memory serves me right, Consivayae was, at that time, the most cherished of all the women at her brothel. The Golden Lai'zen was her domain—a place of both decadence and discretion, reserved for the wealthiest of men, monarchs, and affluent travelers who passed through its gilded doors daily.

We stood in the market for what felt like hours, our conversation weaving between the realities of her life and the stark contrasts of my own. Her words were like a siren's call, painting a picture of a world where even a marked witch might find sanctuary, not in the shadows, but within the very heart of sin. And slowly, she convinced me to accompany her.

FIVE

The Golden Lai'zen was a marvel of opulence, its walls draped in fine fabrics, each curtain pulled to the side by chains of gleaming gold. The floors were covered in rugs so finely woven they seemed almost too precious to tread upon, yet they bore the marks of countless footsteps—those of men seeking pleasure, and women offering it. The men who lounged within were handsome, yet peculiar to me, for in this place, it was not just men of flesh who found refuge, but creatures of all kinds. The Golden Lai'zen welcomed any man, beast, or being, turning away none who had the wealth to pay. Even the feared Gail's of Judgment—the city's enforcers of law and order—turned a blind eye to the sins committed within the walls. They were offered free access to any woman they desired, so long as they kept the peace and left the brothel's owner untroubled.

That owner was a man named Jimford Basoclaz. He was unlike the other brothel keepers in the city, whose cruelty often matched their greed. Jimford, in his way, was a kind man. He believed that a well-treated whore was a woman who would willingly lie on her back, and his philosophy seemed to hold true. He paid his girls a fair share of their earnings, a rarity in a world where women were so often exploited and discarded. In his house, they were not merely property but partners in a profitable venture, and it was this respect, however unconventional, that made the Golden Lai'zen a place of both indulgence and power.

As Consivayae led me through the brothel's lavish halls, I could not help but feel a strange mixture of unease and intrigue. This was a world far removed from the one I had known—a world where power was measured not by the strength of one's arm, but by the allure of one's flesh, where beauty, silence, and the body itself were not just tools of survival but instruments of dominance. And as I stepped deeper into this domain, I couldn't shake the feeling that, for better or worse, my life was about to change in ways I could never have imagined.

He examined me with the practiced eye of a man who had seen countless girls come through his doors, each one hoping to find a place within the walls of his establishment. His rough thumbs brushed over my still-developing breasts, and I suppressed a shiver as he ran his fingers through my hair. But his touch faltered, and he cursed softly as his fingers tangled in the coiled strands. The tight, untamed curls of my mane were foreign to him, a stark contrast to the sleek, straight hair of most of his other girls.

Baso, as he was often called, circled me like a predator assessing its prey. He murmured that he would consider taking me on, but only if Consivayae vouched for me. His gaze lingered on my deep tan skin, the rich hue that set me apart from the others, and he noted with a sly grin the wild, lion-like mane that framed my face. I remember him saying that my youth would sell as well, if not better, than Consivayae herself, the woman who had brought me to him.

At the time, I was naïve, foolish even, and I took his words as a compliment. There was a part of me that swelled with pride, flattered by his approval, blind to the reality of what those words truly meant. I was just a stupid little thing then, desperate for a place in a world that seemed determined to strip me of all dignity. And in that moment, I believed that this was the best choice I had.

The promise of never going hungry again was too tempting to ignore. The assurance of protection from his guards if anyone tried to harm me was a comfort I had long been without. I was tired of being vulnerable, of living in fear that the next day might bring a new peril I was unprepared to face.

So I accepted his offer, not realizing that in doing so, I was trading one kind of danger for another. But I was young, and in my innocence, I believed that within the walls of the Golden Lai'zen, I might finally find the security I had always craved. Little did I know, the path I had chosen would lead me deeper into the shadows than I had ever imagined, where the true price of survival would be revealed in ways I could never have foreseen.

He took me in, handing me five paipeium—the golden coins of the realm that gleamed with the promise of a new life. In that moment, I felt richer than I had ever imagined possible. The weight of those coins in my hand was heavy with possibility, and my heart raced with a mixture of excitement and trepidation. Years ago, I had glimpsed a single paipeium when the late Queen Raye'Zore had taken me to the markets, and it had seemed like a treasure from a distant world. Now, I held five of them in my palm, and the world itself seemed to open before me.

Overwhelmed with gratitude, I ran back to my previous employer, the man who had given me work when few others would. I thanked him profusely, placing one of the golden coins in his hand—a small token of my appreciation for his kindness. His eyes widened in surprise, but he smiled warmly and told me that his doors would always remain open to me, should I ever need to return. His offer was sincere, a rare gift in a world where loyalty was often bought and sold as easily as flesh.

We exchanged our final goodbyes, and with a heart both heavy and bright, I turned my back on that chapter of my life. The future stretched out before me, uncertain but full of potential. I was stepping into a new world, one where I would learn the craft of whoring—a skill as ancient as time, yet one I knew little of beyond whispered rumors and veiled glances.

The path ahead was daunting, but I had made my choice. In the opulent halls of the Golden Lai'zen, I would find my place, learning the art of seduction and survival in a world that prized both. I had traded the security of my former life for something far more unpredictable, and as I walked toward my new fate, I could only hope that I had made the right decision. The weight of those five paipeium in my pocket was a reminder of what I had gained—and of all that I stood to lose.

SIX

In my new home, life took on a strange and intoxicating rhythm. I was provided with three full meals a day, a luxury I had not known in some time, and given free access to as much wine as I could drink. There was also the pa'iku, a wild herb with a dark reputation—one that many in the region used to drown their sorrows or escape their pasts. Its effects were potent, dangerous even; if you inhaled too much, you could pass out, and with each excessive use, a part of your memory could be lost forever. But despite the risks, or perhaps because of them, many people indulged in it, including me.

At first, I was ignorant of its use, fumbling with the herb like a child playing with fire. But one of the other women in the house, whom I soon began to consider my sister, took me under her wing. She, too, was versed in the Sanguine Arts, a practitioner like myself, though I had not realized it at first. Under her guidance, I learned the rituals and techniques that formed the foundation of our shared craft, weaving blood and memory into the very fabric of our lives.

It was Consivayae—who I eventually began to call Rose— who taught me the secrets of the herb, showing me how to mix pa'iku with other plants to create blends that could ease our pain or blur the edges of our minds. Together, we would journey down that hazy path, inhaling the smoke to selectively erase the memories that haunted us. Each session was a dance with oblivion, a careful balancing act between release and forgetting too much.

Finally, one evening, emboldened by the closeness we had cultivated, I found the courage to confide in Rose. I told her of the darkness that had followed me long before we met, the shadows of my past that I had tried so desperately to escape. As I spoke, she listened without judgment, her eyes filled with an understanding that only those who have suffered can offer. In that moment, we became more than sisters in service; we became sisters in spirit, bound by the secrets we shared and the scars we bore.

Rose had her own burdens, too. She spoke of her younger sister, Nora, who had been taken as a mistress by a lord in the distant reaches of Jazzeer. The pain of that separation still lingered in her voice, a reminder that even in a life as seemingly liberated as ours, the past could never truly be erased, only softened by the smoke of pa'iku and the bond of sisterhood.

In those days, as we drifted together through the fog of memory and forgetfulness, I began to understand that the true power of the Sanguine Arts lay not just in the blood or the rituals, but in the connections we forged with those who shared our burdens. And though I had lost much, in Rose, I had found something invaluable—a kindred soul who knew the same depths of sorrow, and who would walk with me through whatever trials lay ahead.

She was taken aback when she first heard the tale of my past—a history steeped in sorrow and shadows. With an urgency born of love and concern, she implored me to cast aside the weight of my tragic memories, to sever the ties that bound me to the pain. I had tried, oh how I had tried, yet each attempt to break free ended in failure. Every night, as we found solace in each other's presence, the thought would creep back into my mind, like a relentless tide against the shore. But soon, I came to a stark realization—I did not want to let it go. That day, etched in the deepest recesses of my soul, was a wound I chose to keep open, a scar I refused to heal. I needed it to remain vivid, a constant reminder that vengeance was still mine to claim.

In time, she understood, and the once-dependable herb we had used to dull our emotions was set aside. We no longer sought its numbing embrace. Instead, we turned inward, sharing our fears and desires, laying bare our souls in the quiet moments between dusk and dawn. And with that, the bond between us deepened.

But the hour had arrived for me to fulfill the purpose for which I was brought here. Nearly two fortnights had passed since I had taken up this mantle, and my coin purse had grown light. It was time, at last, to prove my worth—to earn my keep in a world that demanded more than mere survival.

I felt a thrill course through me, a newfound confidence lighting up my spirit like never before. To say I was prepared would be a gross understatement—I was more than ready. For the past four weeks, I had been meticulously trained in the art of pleasure, learning how to fulfill the desires of men—and beasts, should the need arise. Each client had their own peculiarities, their own cravings, but one truth held firm across them all. Two wet, tight holes—sometimes three, if the client's purse was heavy enough. Yet, more often than not, two sufficed. One for fucking, and one for screaming.

It was a common pursuit for men to seek out women whose voices could shatter the quiet of the night. Their wealthy companions would boast over tea about the screams they could coax from their whores, as if it were some grand sport. Little did they know, we were merely playing our part, performing the role expected of us. Few of us, if any, found genuine pleasure in the cocks we rode for the evening.

Rose and I stood against a shadowed wall, sharing whispered jests about the men who paraded through our doors. Many were handsome, with looks that varied from the tall and imposing to the short and stout, from the robust to the sickly thin. But there was one man in particular, a frequent visitor, who had become almost a fixture in our lives. He was corpulent and self-satisfied, with a stench that clung to him—an odious mix of unwashed flesh and stale wine. His breath reeked of the women he had ravaged, and he had bid for me time and again, offering sums that others might have found tempting.

But not I.

This man would not be the one to claim my first experience as a harlot. No, I wanted something more—a man of beauty, someone who bore even a passing resemblance to the prince of my long-lost dreams. I had the power now—the power to choose who would touch me, when they would touch me, and the price they would pay to enter my rare and sacred temple.

The two of us stood in quiet observation as the lower-ranking girls swayed and gyrated, their oiled bodies glistening in the dim light, bound in chains that clinked to the rhythm of the drums. The air in the brothel was thick, saturated with the scent of pheromones, musk, sweat, and raw, unfiltered desire. It was an intoxicating blend that permeated everything, making the atmosphere heady and almost unbearable. But then, like a breath of fresh air, the scent shifted as Baso's hunters made their entrance, carrying with them a golden-plated fa'ra'fet. The wild boar sizzled atop their shoulders, surrounded by honied apples and roasted potatoes, the aroma of the feast momentarily overpowering the base urges that hung in the air. The night had transformed into a revelry fit for kings—men who were treated as gods, while we, their humble nymphs, catered to their every whim.

I watched as Rose caught the eye of one of her regulars, a man whose presence she had grown accustomed to. He beckoned her with a wave and a swing of his purse, the heavy coins jingling with the promise of a profitable night. She leaned in close, pressing her lips softly against mine, a brief farewell before she was lost to the dancing throng. "Don't wait up," she whispered, a sly smile on her lips, and then she was gone, straddling his lap in mere moments. I watched as she bared her breasts, offering them to his eager mouth. His lips found her nipple, and she arched her head back, moaning, laughing, embodying every lesson she had ever taught me. Rose knew how to make a man burn with desire, and though I had yet to voice it, she had a similar effect on me. Her presence, her touch, had a way of making my thighs slick with unspoken longing.

As the crowd moved and shifted around me, I let my eyes wander over the remaining men, those who prowled about, inspecting the women in chains like cattle at market. None of them stirred anything within me until my gaze landed on two figures who stood out from the rest. I wasn't looking for just any man—I wanted a beast, something wild and untamed, a stallion to ride until he was drenched and spent.

I lingered in the shadows, biding my time, until the two men finally ducked through the doorway. They were massive, their heads brushing the low-hanging beams as they entered. Both wore silver armor adorned with a crest I had never seen before—a red hound's head encased in flames, with a sword driven deep into its skull. Warriors, that much was clear, and their presence stirred something primal within me. I had heard tales that there was no better cock than one saved for the victory of battle.

The first of the two had hair the color of autumn leaves, a rich copper that caught the light, his pale skin a stark contrast to the vibrant hue. His eyes were sharp, piercing, and they seemed to see through flesh and bone, straight to the heart of a woman. His companion, however, intrigued me even more. His skin was a warm, light brown, his eyes a molten gold that shone with a predatory gleam. Long black hair cascaded down to the middle of his back, with the ends dipped in a deep green, like the last remnants of summer clinging to the night. There was an arrogance to him, a confidence that bordered on egotism, and I found myself drawn to it.

Out of the pair, it was the first who captivated my attention, his presence commanding and impossible to ignore. This was the beast I sought—a creature of power and strength, one who would challenge me, and in turn, be brought to his knees by my touch. The night was still young, and I had yet to choose. But as I watched the two of them, I knew that my decision had already been made.

Women flocked around them like moths drawn to a flame, their laughter and eager hands competing for the attention of the two towering warriors. I couldn't understand why—these men were strangers, yet they seemed to command a reverence reserved for legends. I watched from the shadows, patience guiding my every move as I waited for the perfect moment. Finally, I slipped through the throng, weaving between bodies until I stood before them. My gaze locked with the copper-haired warrior, and a devious smile curled his lips, as if he had known all along that I would choose him. I offered myself with a sultry tilt of my head, and he accepted with a nod, his eyes gleaming with anticipation. But his companion was not as pleased.

"So, you're a girl of sand and summer flesh, yet you extend your tight little cunt to a male of the ice," he sneered, his golden eyes narrowing with disdain.

"Summer flesh" was a term meant to categorize people like him and me, a label rooted in the twisted hierarchy of our world. The arctic's were those of nearly milk-white skin, cold and distant like the lands they hailed from. Then came the pale, the rust, the summer flesh, and finally the sindust—each title a relic of the war that had fractured our lands, a crude attempt to define who posed a threat and who was allowed to live in peace.

Tyliquin witches, like me, often fell somewhere between rust and sindust, our complexions marking us as dangerous, our very existence an affront to those who clung to their flawed beliefs. The darker your skin, the greater the threat you were perceived to be. It was a twisted logic, devoid of true value, yet they clung to it with a fervor that defied reason.

I cast a few playful jests into the air between us, letting them linger like the scent of forbidden fruit. But I had made my choice, and no amount of prejudice or scorn would sway me. The copper-haired warrior was mine tonight, and I intended to enjoy every moment of it.

With a confident stride, I led him away from the crowded hall, past the curious gazes and whispered remarks, until we reached the privacy of my chambers. The heavy door closed behind us with a finality that sent a thrill through my veins. Here, in this secluded space, the power was mine. I would take this man of the ice and melt him with the heat of my summer flesh, until he was nothing more than a breathless whisper on my lips.

He paid in full, the clinking of coins against my palm a promise of the night to come. As the last piece of gold settled, I began to undress him, peeling away layers of cloth to reveal the truth hidden beneath. His body was a canvas of scars, each one a story of battles fought and won, but it was the texture of his skin that truly caught my attention. It was tougher than any human's, a hardness that I had only felt twice before. My breath hitched as the realization dawned—this man, who had intrigued me so deeply, was not a man at all. He was a shifter in disguise, a hidden dragon who had wandered into our world.

For weeks, I had prayed, naked and on bended knee, that my first true encounter would be with a dragon bold enough to venture into our brothel. The gods had listened, answering my prayers in the form of this warrior. We came together in a kiss that was fierce, filled with hunger and a burning passion that consumed us both. He pushed me onto the bed with a strength that sent a thrill through my entire being, and as he hovered over me, my mind drifted away from the brothel. I was no longer in that dimly lit room; I was back in the small cottage where I had first become one with Calira, the lover I had lost.

As he entered me, a low moan escaped my lips, the feeling of his girth stirring memories of a love that had once been mine. He moved within me, each thrust a reminder of the pleasure I had once known, a pleasure I thought lost forever. But soon, the rhythm of our coupling ignited a feral hunger within me, a need to take control.

With a growl, I pushed him off and flipped him onto the furs, taking a moment to truly admire the form of the dragon before me. In those days, the body of a hidden dragon was not so different from that of a human. He appeared as a man in nearly every way, save for a few telltale signs. His cock, his ears, and his eyes betrayed his true nature. His skin, though soft to the touch, concealed scales that could be felt if one dug their nails in deep enough. His ears were pointed and sharp, and his eyes gleamed with a serpentine intensity that sent shivers down my spine.

I trailed my tongue down his body, savoring the taste of him, until I reached the pointed tip of his manhood. As I took him into my mouth, his moans deepened, his hand fisting in my hair as I brought him to the brink. It wasn't long before he found release, his body shuddering as I swallowed every drop of the pleasure he had paid for. But in my mind, it was not this drake who lay beneath me—it was Calira, his talons digging into the bed linens as he spread his legs for me one last time.

When it was over, he handed me an entire purse of golden coins, far more than I had expected. He dressed quickly, gathering his things with a quiet efficiency, but before he left, he turned to me with a promise on his lips. He would visit again, he said, though when exactly, he could not know.

As I cleaned myself up and closed my services for the evening, I couldn't help but feel a flicker of hope. I had earned nearly three days' pay for a single night, but more than that, I had tasted true pleasure—a pleasure I had only ever known with one other dragon. For a brief, fleeting moment, I allowed myself to hope that he would stay true to his word and return to me. But in the world I lived in, hopes were dangerous things, and I knew better than to hold onto them for too long.

SEVEN

The weeks that followed my initiation into the world of harlotry were anything but ordinary. Business slowed to a crawl, a stark contrast to the fervor of my first night. Many of our regular patrons had been summoned to war, their absence casting a shadow over the once-bustling brothel. The looming threat of the traitorous Halotia's Covenant had struck fear into the hearts of all, especially those who ruled the skies with fire and wings. The foreign warriors had begun their campaign of terror, not only in Crystal Springs but across the outlying islands scattered over the Maiden's Sea.

The leader of this fearsome force was a creature known as the Mist, a hound of Drathell who, at the time, was more legend than flesh. He and his ruthless pack had claimed Dragon's Bane Fortress as their stronghold, a formidable castle nestled within the forests and hills of Halotia's Havoc. This vast, untamed landscape lay within the borders of Aleanthos, a country now steeped in blood and war. The dragons, proud rulers of the sky, were being slaughtered by the thousands, their blood staining the earth in rivers of crimson. Many were felled in cold blood, their lives extinguished by the cruelty of men and their unrelenting hunger for power.

Rumors swirled like the thick mist that often clung to the city's edges—whispers that our own city would soon be the next target of the covenant's wrath. Such tales often flowed from the lips of drunken men, their words slurred with dreams of glory and the thrill of impending battle. Yet, despite the bravado, a thread of genuine fear wove through their stories, a fear I could not easily dismiss.

Amidst the uncertainty, my thoughts often drifted to Calira. Though we had been separated by circumstance and duty, my worry for him was a constant companion. Calira was no ordinary dragon; he was the prince of Crystal Springs, a ruler destined to protect his people. If war came to our city, he would be there, on the front lines, his life hanging in the balance. The thought of him facing the Mist and his mutts sent a shiver down my spine, a chill that no amount of warmth could chase away.

The world outside the brothel's walls was changing, growing darker with each passing day. The once-safe haven of Crystal Springs now felt precarious, as if teetering on the edge of an abyss. And yet, amidst the fear and uncertainty, there remained a flicker of hope, a belief that Calira would survive this war and return to me. But hope was a fragile thing, easily shattered, and I knew better than to cling too tightly to it.

Still, in the quiet moments, when the brothel was empty and the night stretched long, I allowed myself to dream of his return. A dream where the war would end, the Covenant would fall, and the prince of Crystal Springs would once again soar above his city, victorious and unscathed. But until that day, all I could do was wait, my heart heavy with a worry that would not leave.

I spent my days in preparation, gathering supplies and storing them away in secret, knowing that the time would come when my adopted sister and I would be forced to flee the city and survive on what the land could offer. When I wasn't on my back, enduring the quick and clumsy thrusts of some boy who lacked the stamina to truly satisfy, I was planning our escape. The other whores who shared the brothel with me were blind to the looming danger. They mocked me, making me the center of every joke, calling me paranoid for my caution and meticulous planning. Their laughter only fueled my resolve, for I knew the day of reckoning was drawing near.

And when that day finally arrived, the satisfaction I felt was bittersweet. The warning came not in the form of a prophecy or omen, but in the frantic pounding of a familiar fist on our door. It was a young man, one who had made our brothel his second home, much to the dismay of his wife. He had been one of my most frequent clients, though he wasn't shy about spreading his affections among the other women. Yet it was my dark skin that kept him returning to me, night after night, his lustful eyes always seeking me out in the crowded rooms.

His wife had not taken kindly to his frequent visits. She had confronted me once, bursting into the brothel with fire in her eyes, her voice shrill with anger and pain. She had called me a demoness, a mistress of Dovium himself, her words dripping with the venom of a woman scorned. It was a common refrain among small-minded fools like her, to blame the color of my skin for their husbands' infidelities, as if I were some sorceress who had bewitched him, rather than a woman who simply knew how to give him what he craved. Her insults had rolled off me like water on stone, for I knew the truth. It was not my fault that she was nothing more than a frigid girl, incapable of holding onto the affections of a man who sought warmth elsewhere.

Now, that same man stood at our door, his face pale and his eyes wide with terror. The day I had long predicted had arrived, and with it, the time to leave this place behind. While the other whores scurried about in panic, their laughter at my expense forgotten in the face of real danger, I felt a cold sense of satisfaction. I had been right to prepare, to plan, and now I would be the one to lead my sister and myself to safety, while the rest were left to face the consequences of their foolishness.

I wasted no time. Gathering the supplies I had so carefully hoarded, I took my sister by the hand, and together we slipped into the night, leaving the brothel and its doomed inhabitants behind. The city that had once been our home was now a battleground, and only those who had the foresight to prepare would survive. As we made our way through the darkened streets, the sounds of chaos growing louder behind us, I couldn't help but think of the young wife who had cursed me. Perhaps she was right to fear me, after all. For in the end, it wasn't just her husband's heart that I had taken—it was her future, as well.

I have always believed that there is no fury more potent, more consuming, than that of a woman betrayed by the very man she is bound to serve. My suspicions about her had been correct all along. Until that fateful night, Arobren had stood as an impenetrable fortress. Our walls were strong, fortified by the sweat and blood of those who sought to protect us. Warriors guarded every gate, and strict laws forbade anyone from entering or leaving the city after dusk. We had taken every precaution, every measure to ensure our safety. But all of that crumbled when the adulterer's wife decided to wield her power in the most treacherous way.

Between her legs she had ensnared the heart of a young guard, a boy barely more than a child, newly inducted into King Raye'Zore's ranks. He was inexperienced, both in battle and in the ways of the world, and his naivety made him an easy target for her wiles. She had used the promise of her body, the sweet allure of a wet cunt, to twist his mind and bend his will to her desires. Like any youth intoxicated by the pleasures of the flesh, he was quick to fall under her spell, and in his foolishness, he handed over the keys to the city gates—keys meant to keep us safe from the very danger she sought to invite in.

From what I gathered, she had spun a tale of woe, claiming to be a victim of her husband's cruelty, desperate to escape his abusive grasp under the cover of night. She pleaded for the guard's help, her eyes brimming with false tears, her voice laced with a tremor that spoke of fear and desperation. The boy, caught between his duty and the seductive pull of her request, chose the path of betrayal. Little did he know, the woman he sought to save was meeting not with freedom, but with the Mist himself.

In her treachery, she had paved the way for our downfall, opening the gates to our enemies, all in the name of revenge. She had sold not only her body but the lives of every soul within Arobren to satisfy her fury. And for what? The fleeting satisfaction of seeing her husband suffer? In her twisted logic, she believed that betraying us all would somehow right the wrongs done to her. But in truth, she had condemned us to a fate far worse.

That night, the city's defenses were undone not by the might of an army but by the lust of a foolish boy and the vengeance of a scorned woman. As the Mist and his forces swept through the city, I couldn't help but wonder if she realized the gravity of her actions. Did she understand that her thirst for retribution had cost so many their lives? Or was she blinded by her rage, her heart too consumed by hatred to see the devastation she had wrought?

One thing was certain: the fury of a betrayed woman is a force to be reckoned with, but in this case, it had become a weapon of mass destruction. Arobren had been betrayed not by an outsider, but from within, by one of our own. And as the city fell to ruin, I could only curse the day that boy had been so easily swayed, and the night that woman had chosen to wield her fury like a dagger to our throats.

I will never forget that night. I was in the bath, my hands lost in the endless struggle to tame the unruly coils of my hair, when my master burst into the room, his chest heaving, sweat streaming down his face. His eyes were wide with terror, and his voice cracked with desperation as he shouted, "We have to run! We have to go now! The Covenant—they've found a way to cross the water!"

The urgency in his voice sent a jolt of fear through me. I leaped from the tub, my skin freezing as the chilled air bit into my wet, naked body. The world outside was crumbling, and I was unprepared. As I stumbled into the main room, I found Rose, her head thrown back, her mouth wrapped around the length of a man lost in his own pleasure. Without a second thought, I grabbed her by the hair, yanking her away from him and urging her to move.

Panic clawed at my throat, but I forced it down, knowing we had no time to waste.

We dashed down to the cellar, where we had been secretly hoarding supplies, our only chance of survival should the worst come to pass. I pulled on a simple gown, the fabric sticking to my damp skin, and turned to climb the stairs when a sharp, searing pain knifed through my stomach. The intensity of it nearly brought me to my knees, but I clung to the railing, refusing to succumb. Rose was at my side in an instant, helping me to regain my balance, but then the ground beneath us trembled, sending us both sprawling.

Above, chaos reigned. The sounds of panic and terror echoed through the brothel as naked men and women ran in every direction, their screams mingling with the thunder of footsteps. The front door was suddenly kicked open, and a flood of men poured into the room. But these were not the usual warriors who visited our establishment. No, these men were draped in holy white cloth, each hem adorned with gold, their appearance almost blinding in its sanctimonious purity.

I watched in horror as they descended upon us, slaughtering my sisters in the name of their so-called righteousness. Blood sprayed across the vibrant satin of their robes, the crimson staining the purity they claimed to uphold. Rose and I stood frozen, paralyzed by the brutality unfolding before our eyes. But when one of the men spotted us, we snapped into action, turning on our heels and fleeing. Our feet barely touched the ground as we ran, but another of the invaders had already closed in, his sword leveled at our throats.

In that moment, something inside me snapped. A fire ignited in my veins, a lust for blood and a hunger for vengeance that I had never known before. Without thinking, I dropped to the ground, swinging my fist up into his groin with all the force I could muster. He crumpled to the floor, a pitiful whimper escaping his lips. Seizing the opportunity, I snatched his sword, positioning myself between Rose and the second man who approached with murderous intent.

Together, we fought him off, Rose grabbing hold of his weapon when we finally disarmed him. With no time to waste, we fled through a side door, the night air biting at our skin as we burst into the streets. The city was a nightmare—flashes of black fur streaked past us, the mauling's of beasts adding to the chaos. The cries of women echoed in my ears, their bodies thrown over their children in a desperate attempt to protect them. It was a haunting sound, one that would linger in my mind for years to come.

The men who should have been their protectors had abandoned them, leaving them to fend for themselves. The failures of that night weighed heavily on me, but there was no time to grieve, no time to mourn. We had to survive. We had to keep moving.

The brothel, the city, everything we had known was lost to the flames of war and the cruelty of men who believed they held righteousness in their hands. But as we fled, swords in hand and blood in our veins, I knew that we would not go down without a fight. That night marked the end of one life and the beginning of another—a life forged in the fires of vengeance, with a will to survive stronger than any blade that could be wielded against us.

"We're not going to make it out of here alive, Tonisa!" Rose's voice trembled as she clung to me, her grip desperate. In that moment, I felt the weight of her terror, as if she believed that I alone could save her from the nightmare unfolding around us. I turned, casting my gaze over my shoulder toward the horizon. There, in the thin line where sky met earth, I saw it—a silhouette against the darkening sky, unmistakable in its form. A dragon.

As I watched, the shape grew clearer, closer, and then I saw them—three more, flanking the first in perfect formation. They flew with purpose, their wings beating in a rhythm that sent ripples through the air. My heart surged with hope, a glimmer of salvation in the midst of chaos. Rose, too, had caught sight of them, her wide eyes reflecting the same desperate hope that filled me.

"We have to go! We have to hide! If we can survive until they reach us, we might live through this!" I urged her, my voice fierce with determination.

Without another word, we ran, our feet pounding the earth, hearts racing as we sought refuge. We found it in a house that had already been reduced to ruin, its walls crumbling, a mere shadow of what it once was. We dove beneath a pile of hay, clutching each other tightly, our bodies trembling with both fear and the faintest glimmer of hope. We whispered our prayers to whatever gods might be listening, begging them to grant us just a little more time—time for the dragons to reach us, to save us from the hell that had descended upon our city.

The ground beneath us shook, a deep, unsettling tremor that rattled our bones. For several agonizing moments, we didn't know the cause of the tremors, our imaginations conjuring every possible horror. I couldn't stay hidden; I had to know what was happening. Carefully, I lifted my head, peeking out through a broken window, and then I saw him. The Mist.

He stood just outside the ruins we had taken shelter in, a figure of terrifying power and presence. He was larger than I had ever imagined, towering nearly as tall as the dragons I had known since childhood. Yet, he was leaner, more agile, his movements almost impossible to track. There was an eerie grace to him, a fluidity that belied his immense size. His very presence made the air thick with dread.

Then, without a single movement, he vanished. One moment he was there, and the next he was gone, leaving nothing but the trembling earth in his wake. The ground shook again, and this time it was followed by a sound that sent a shiver of both fear and longing through me—the long, guttural roar of dragons. It was a sound that had once been a part of my everyday life, a comfort in the sky, and yet, I had missed it so terribly during these endless nights of uncertainty and fear. The king's forces had arrived.

The roar of the dragons filled the air, powerful and commanding, a promise of retribution and salvation. The hope that had been a fragile thing now flared into something stronger, something that could sustain us through the terror of the moment. The Mist might be a force to reckon with, but so were the dragons that now soared overhead, their presence a beacon of hope in a world gone mad.

As we huddled together beneath the hay, the sounds of battle began to echo through the city, the clash of steel and the roar of fire filling the air. For the first time in what felt like an eternity, I dared to believe that we might survive this night, that we might live to see another dawn. But even as that hope blossomed within me, I knew that the fight was far from over. The Mist was still out there, somewhere in the shadows, and the battle had only just begun.

EIGHT

R ose and I scrambled to our feet, rushing to the window to
see who Ramsra had sent to defend his people. As we
peered out, a massive cloud of darkness swept over the small
cottage where we had sought refuge. It blotted out the light,
casting everything in shadow, and suddenly, that familiar, searing
pain returned to my belly. It was unlike anything I had ever felt, a
burning ache that pulled me into a trance. Rose's frantic voice
reached out to me, her hands shaking my shoulders, trying
desperately to bring me back to my senses. But her words fell on
deaf ears; I was no longer in control of my own body.

Compelled by a force beyond my understanding, I walked
out of the cottage, my eyes fixed on the creature that filled the
sky. The massive winged serpent—no, it was more than a mere
serpent, it was a dragon of unimaginable size and power—
hovered above us, its form casting a long, terrifying shadow over

the city. His body stretched across rows of houses, his wings spreading as wide as the lake at the city's heart. His chest and underbelly gleamed with armor, meticulously crafted to protect him in battle, while his silky mane, braided into thick cords, hung far beneath the mighty arch of his throat.

The dragon flew with grace and lethal purpose, all four of his limbs tucked safely beneath his immense body. It wasn't until he unleashed a torrent of flame upon the city that I truly saw the scope of his power. The fire erupted from his maw with the force of thunder, a blaze so fierce that it consumed everything in its path—men, women, children, and hellhounds alike. The ground quaked under the might of his attack, and the air filled with the stench of burning flesh and the screams of the dying.

As the dragon banked in the sky, my breath caught in my throat. There, perched safely on the beast's back, was King Raye'Zore, his presence unmistakable even from a distance. But it was not the king who held my gaze—it was the dragon. For in that moment, as the flames licked the stone and the city burned, I recognized him. It was Calira, my lost love, and his bastard of a father, united in destruction.

A rush of conflicting emotions surged through me, a torrent of fear, pride, and an undeniable, primal arousal. My body reacted before my mind could comprehend it. The power that radiated from Calira was intoxicating, a force so overwhelming that it left me trembling with excitement. I had known him, loved him, made him mine. And now, seeing him in his full, fearsome glory, a being of such unimaginable power and terror, a surge of pride welled up inside me—a pride I had never known I was capable of feeling.

I had loved this creature, this dragon who now rained destruction upon the city. I had held his heart in my hands, controlled it, shaped it, and now he was here, larger than life, more fearsome than I could have ever imagined. Even as chaos reigned around me, even as the city burned and lives were lost, I could not tear my gaze away from him. I had been a part of this— of him—and the knowledge filled me with a twisted sense of satisfaction, a pride that bordered on madness.

In the midst of all the death and destruction, I was reminded of the bond we had shared, of the nights when he had been mine, of the power I had once wielded over him. And though the world around me was falling apart, there was a small, dark corner of my soul that reveled in the sight of him, in the destruction he wrought, and in the knowledge that I had once been the one to bring this mighty dragon to his knees.

Rose rushed outside to join me, but before we could take another step, we were thrown to the ground by the turbulent wake of a giant white dragon. The force of its passing was so powerful that it sent us sprawling, and we could do nothing but crawl across the street, desperately seeking shelter. We finally braced ourselves against a wall, hidden in a narrow alley, our hearts pounding as the chaos raged around us.

Above, two more dragons flew past, their scales gleaming in the firelight. One was a vibrant green and gold, its wings cutting through the air with effortless grace. The other was a blinding bronze, its body reflecting the flames that consumed the city below. As I watched them soar, a realization struck me like a bolt of lightning. My mind flashed back to the night I had spent with the copper-haired warrior, to the connection we had shared. The pieces of the puzzle suddenly fell into place—the dragons flying above us were not just any dragons. They were the very men I had encountered before, transformed into their true, fearsome forms.

I pulled myself to my feet, my breath catching in my throat as the magnitude of the situation sank in. Rose, sensing my urgency, followed without question as we ran toward the west gate, now engulfed in flames. The world around us was a cacophony of destruction, but we pressed on, driven by the desperate need to escape.

We crossed the threshold of the city and plunged into the wild embrace of nature beyond the walls, but something made me stop in my tracks. An unsettling tremor coursed through the ground beneath us, a warning that something terrible was about to happen. I turned back, my eyes scanning the sky, where only three dragons remained. The bronze serpent was gone, its absence filling me with a sense of dread.

And then I saw him—Calira, my love, diving toward the ground with a roar that shook the heavens. His jaws were wide, a feral and valiant cry escaping his throat, as if he were summoning every ounce of strength for the battle to come. But before he could reach his target, the Mist appeared out of thin air, materializing like a phantom. His massive teeth sank into Calira's neck, the impact so sudden and brutal that it stole the breath from my lungs.

I could only watch, frozen in horror, as the Mist clamped down, his jaws locking onto Calira with merciless precision. Blood spilled from the wound, a deep crimson that stained the sky as Calira struggled against his attacker. The world seemed to slow, the sounds of battle fading into a dull roar as my heart pounded in my ears.

This was the moment I had dreaded, the moment I had prayed would never come. My lover, the mighty dragon who had once been mine, was now caught in the clutches of the hellhound that would destroy all. His strength, his power, all that he was, was being drained away by the beast that had brought so much destruction to our world.

Desperation clawed at me, but I was powerless to help him. All I could do was stand there, tears streaming down my face, as the love of my life fought for his very existence. And in that moment, I realized that the bond we had shared, the love that had once been so strong, might not be enough to save him from the darkness that had descended upon us.

The pair plummeted from the sky, the Mist clinging to Calira with a ferocity that made my heart stop. As they spiraled downward, a small white-headed speck was thrown from Calira's back—it was the king. My breath caught as I watched him fall, and though the thought was treasonous, I found myself praying that he would meet his end on the unforgiving ground below.

But even as the king tumbled to what I hoped was his death, Calira fought to right himself. With a powerful beat of his wings, he managed to level his descent, though his landing was anything but graceful. He crashed onto his feet with a force that shook the earth, the impact sending shockwaves through the city and into the depths of my soul. The hound released him, their bodies separating as they both took a moment to regain their balance.

I will never forget the way they faced each other in those final moments—two colossal beings, locked in a battle that would decide the fate of everything. Even from a distance, I could feel the raw aggression radiating from them, their hatred almost tangible. They were giants, their every movement filled with deadly intent.

And then, just as suddenly as he had appeared, the hound vanished again, disappearing into the shadows like a ghost. The ground fell eerily silent, the echoes of their battle fading into the distance. For a moment, all was still, as if the world itself held its breath, waiting to see who would emerge victorious.

Rose and I knew better than to stay and find out. With the earth still trembling beneath our feet, we turned and fled into the forest, seeking refuge among the ancient trees. The woods became our sanctuary, the only place we could think to hide until the dust settled and the fate of the city was decided.

We moved quickly, the sounds of battle fading behind us as we ventured deeper into the safety of the wild. The forest, with its towering trees and thick underbrush, offered us shelter and a semblance of peace. Here, we could wait, our ears straining for any sign of the outcome. We knew that until we heard word of who had claimed victory—whether it was Calira or the Mist—we could not return to what remained of our lives.

The woods would be our home, a place of uncertainty and fear, but also of hope. For as long as we remained hidden among the trees, there was still a chance that Calira would survive, that he would find his way back to me. And until that day came, Rose and I would wait, our fates intertwined with the battle that raged far beyond the forest's edge.

NINE

Thirty-two days—Rose and I survived in the woods for thirty-two days, living off the land and the meager supplies we had managed to gather. On the thirty-third day, everything changed. My life, already shattered by the events of the past weeks, took a turn I had never anticipated. I was with child.

At first, I tried to deny it, pushing the thought away as if it were a shadow that could be banished with the light of reason. But my body told me otherwise. The signs were undeniable—the fullness in my belly, the aching in my bones, the queasiness that left me swaying with nausea. These were sensations only a woman could understand, ancient and primal, a connection to life that transcended fear and logic.

It wasn't until I truly allowed myself to feel that I realized what had been hiding in the chaos. Over two months had passed since my last bleeding, and my breasts had grown so tender that even the gentle touch of water during a bath caused me pain. For a brief, fleeting moment, I felt a spark of joy. I was going to be a mother. The thought brought a warmth to my heart that I hadn't felt in what seemed like an eternity, a sense of purpose amidst the destruction that had consumed my world.

But that joy was short-lived. The reality of my situation crashed down on me like a wave, washing away any hope I might have nurtured. I realized with cold clarity that I had no way of knowing who the father of this child was. The memories of that night came rushing back—just days before I had welcomed Calira into my body, I had been raped. The two events were so close together that I could never be sure of the truth. I was either carrying the child of the dragon I had loved, my greatest accomplishment, or the offspring of a monster, the bane of my very existence.

The life growing within me must have sensed my inner turmoil, for it made every day a living hell. I was plagued by relentless bouts of vomiting, my balance faltered as if the ground itself were conspiring against me, and exhaustion weighed me down like a leaden shroud. No matter how much I slept, I woke just as tired, my energy sapped by the burden I carried. It was this unyielding misery that led me to a grim conclusion—this had to be Ramsra's child.

Ramsra, the one who had taken my maidenhead, the one who had defiled me in a moment of cruelty. He was older, his bloodline stronger, more ancient, and advanced than his son's. The thought of raising a child conceived in rape, a child who might carry the darkness of his father, filled me with a dread so profound that it left me breathless. I did not want to be shackled with the burden of caring for the offspring of a beast I loathed with every fiber of my being.

And yet, what choice did I have? The child grew within me, indifferent to my fears, a force of life that could not be denied or wished away. Each day I wrestled with the questions that haunted me: Would I be able to love this child if it were Ramsra's? Could I find the strength to raise it, knowing the circumstances of its conception? Or would this child, innocent though it was, be a constant reminder of my suffering, a living embodiment of the cruelty that had been inflicted upon me?

The answers eluded me, and as the days wore on, I felt more lost than ever. The joy I had briefly felt at the thought of motherhood was swallowed by a sea of uncertainty and fear. This was not the life I had imagined for myself, and yet it was the one I had been given. I could only hope that in the end, I would find a way to reconcile the darkness of my past with the future that was now growing within me. But for now, all I could do was endure, one painful, exhausting day at a time.

Desperation drove me to dark places in those early days. I tried everything to rid myself of the child I believed was the spawn of a monster. I hurled myself off a hillside, praying that the violent fall would end the pregnancy, but all I gained were bruises and cuts that burned with a bitter reminder of my failure. My body, battered but not broken, clung to the life within me with a stubbornness that both enraged and terrified me.

When the physical attempts failed, I turned to my knowledge of herbs, diving deep into the dangerous world of poisons and potions. I tried oil of willinth, a substance so potent that it was said to bring even the strongest to their knees. I stuffed leaf of crow inside me, hoping its deadly properties would do what my body would not. But the child remained, resilient, defiant against every effort to end its existence. With each attempt on its life, it seemed only to grow stronger, as if fueled by my hatred.

Eventually, I had to admit defeat. The child was not going anywhere. Rose watched my downward spiral with growing concern, her eyes filled with worry as she tried to comfort me. She clung to the hope that the baby was Calira's, urging me to await its birth with patience and love. But I couldn't share her optimism. The truth was a dark, twisting thing inside me, and no amount of hope could untangle it.

By the time my belly began to swell with the unmistakable signs of pregnancy, we had returned to our city. The ruins had been rebuilt, and life, for the most part, seemed to have resumed its usual rhythm. The whorehouse where we worked was once again bustling with activity, and I returned to my post, though now with a new condition that altered my role. Being a pregnant whore came with its own peculiar set of advantages. Certain men with certain fetishes sought me out, eager to indulge in the taboo of my growing belly. It was work, and it kept my mind from the dark thoughts that still haunted me.

As my pregnancy advanced, I grew too large to service anyone, and the madam allowed me to rest. I spent nearly half a fortnight in bed, my body heavy with the weight of the life I had tried so hard to deny. The rest was a welcome reprieve, but it did little to ease the fear that gnawed at me.

Then, one night, I was jolted awake by a rush of warm liquid between my legs. Panic gripped me as I realized what was happening—my water had broken. The pain followed quickly, a scalding, ripping agony that tore through me with a force that left me gasping for breath. I screamed, the sound raw and animalistic, and within moments, Rose and a few other women were by my side.

I looked down and saw the blood, so much blood, staining the sheets and pooling beneath me. The sight of it filled me with a terror unlike anything I had ever known. I didn't want to die. The stories of women who perished during childbirth flooded my mind, and I feared that I would be just another name added to the list.

The pain was relentless, each contraction a wave of fire that consumed me, leaving me weak and trembling. The women around me did their best to soothe me, but their words were drowned out by the roaring in my ears. All I could do was hold on, my body wracked with pain, as the child I had once tried to kill now fought its way into the world.

In those moments, I was caught between life and death, teetering on the edge as I struggled to bring this child into the light. The blood continued to flow, a crimson river that threatened to take me with it, but I clung to the thin thread of life with all the strength I had left. I didn't want to die. Not like that. Not there.

And so I fought. I fought with every ounce of strength I had, driven by a will to survive that even I hadn't known existed. The room spun, the voices around me faded in and out, but I kept pushing, kept fighting, until finally, with one last, agonizing effort, I felt the child slip from my body.

The pain ebbed, leaving me trembling and weak, but alive. I heard the cries of the newborn, a sharp, piercing wail that cut through the fog of exhaustion that had settled over me. The women around me moved quickly, cleaning and tending to the baby, but all I could do was lie there, staring up at the ceiling, my chest heaving as I tried to catch my breath. I had survived. We had both survived.

But as I lay there, too weak to move, the question that had haunted me from the beginning returned, more insistent than ever. Who was this child? Was it the product of love or of violence?

My greatest accomplishment or my darkest curse? The answers still eluded me, but as I listened to the cries of the life I had brought into the world, I knew that I would have to face them, one way or another.

Seventeen hours—that's how long it took to bring that child into the world. I can still feel every excruciating moment, every inch of my body tearing apart as if I were being split in two. The pain was a relentless, merciless force, and as I labored, there were fleeting moments of lucidity where I prayed to the gods, begging them to grant me a son. A son would have been a symbol of strength, a child I might have been able to accept, to mold into something greater than the circumstances of his birth. But, as with so many of my prayers, the gods were silent.

When the ordeal finally ended, it was not a son that I held in my arms, but a wailing, fat little girl. She was as healthy as any newborn could be, her cries strong and piercing, a leech that had fed off my body for just over eight months, draining me of every resource I had. The relief of delivering her was short-lived, replaced by a deep exhaustion that settled into my bones. I was weak, feeble even. My skin had lost its color, my hair had become dry and brittle, splitting at the ends, and my cunt burned with the aftershocks of what felt like a war waged inside me.

I looked down at the child, her tiny face scrunched in protest at being thrust into the world. I searched her features, desperate to find some trace of Calira or his father, something that would give me a clue as to who had sired her. But there was nothing. She was a bald blank slate, a tiny, helpless being with no clear ties to the men who had left their mark on me.

I couldn't bring myself to love her. She wasn't my child; she was something that had happened to me, an event rather than a person. I didn't give her a name because a name would have meant acceptance, a recognition of her as part of me. Instead, I fed her, fulfilling only the basic obligation of sustenance, because that was all I could offer. She had taken so much from me already—my strength, my will, my very body—and I couldn't bear to give her anything more.

I sent Rose out into the night, tasked with finding someone who would take the child off my hands. It took nearly a week before the answer to my problem walked through the door. I don't remember his name, but I will never forget his face. He was tall, his build gaunt and almost otherworldly, with one golden eye and one green. His hair was impossibly long, trailing behind him as he moved, brushing the floor with each step. His skin was the color of sand, a warm, pale hue that contrasted sharply with the deep, resonant tone of his voice.

There was a certain pride in the way he spoke, a confidence that made it clear he was used to getting what he wanted. He didn't ask questions about the child's origins, nor did he seem concerned with why I was so eager to be rid of her. He simply looked down at her, his mismatched eyes narrowing slightly, and nodded as if this, too, was part of some grand design he alone understood.

I handed her over without a word, feeling nothing as his long fingers closed around the swaddled bundle. She was no longer my burden, no longer my responsibility. She would be another's problem now, her fate tied to the whims of a man I would never see again. As the door closed behind him, I felt an odd mixture of relief and emptiness, as though a part of me had been cut away and cast into the void.

I never spoke of her again. I pushed the memory of her existence deep into the recesses of my mind, locking it away where it couldn't haunt me. In time, the pain would fade, the emptiness would dull, and I would go on living as I always had—surviving, one day at a time. But that night, as I lay in the dark, I couldn't help but wonder what kind of life awaited the child I had given away. Would she grow into something more than what she was—a reminder of pain, of loss, of a life I never wanted?

But the answers to those questions were not mine to seek. She was gone, and with her, I hoped, the ghosts of the past would go too.

Five months slipped by like a fleeting shooting star after the birth of the little bastard whelp. Each day blended into the next, a blur of routine and numbness as I tried to push the past behind me. But then, at the end of those months, the sound of a town crier's voice shattered the fragile peace I had built around myself. He rode through the streets, his voice loud and clear as he announced the news that struck me like a dagger to the heart: Prince Calira Raye'Zore had been married.

My heart plummeted into a chasm of despair, quickly replaced by a seething jealousy so fierce it could have torn Hailotia itself from the heavens. The news was like a poison, spreading through my veins, igniting a fire of rage that threatened to consume me whole. I didn't know who the woman was, the one who had taken what I had once dreamed could be mine, but it didn't matter. All I knew was that I hated her with every fiber of my being. I wanted her dead. I wanted to kill her.

She had everything I had ever desired—a life with Calira, a future that should have been mine. The thought of them together, of her lying in the bed that should have been mine, drove me to the brink of madness. She had taken my place, stolen the life I had fought so hard for, and for that, she would pay.

But I knew I had to be patient. I couldn't let my anger consume me too soon, couldn't act on impulse and risk everything. No, I would wait. I would bide my time, and when the day came, I would be ready. I would find her, and I would make her suffer as I had suffered. I would take back what was mine, and the world would tremble at the force of my wrath.

The future was uncertain, but one thing was clear in my mind: this woman, whoever she was, would not escape my vengeance. She would know the pain of loss, just as I had. And when that day came, I would be there, ready to exact the justice that had been denied to me. The jealousy that burned within me was now my driving force, my reason for enduring each day that passed. It was only a matter of time before the scales would be balanced, and I would have my revenge.

TEN

My life as a whore became increasingly unsatisfying, a hollow existence that only deepened the ache in my heart. The money was good, but it was a poor balm for the grief that had taken root in my soul. The news of Calira and his new bride had shattered me, bringing me to my knees in a sorrow so profound that it crippled me in ways I hadn't anticipated. The facade of submission I had perfected for my work began to crumble, slipping through my fingers like sand.

As a harlot, there were moments of pleasure to be found, the occasional client who knew how to skillfully bring a woman to climax. But even those few had begun to fail me. My body, once a vessel of desire, now rejected them. It wasn't their fault; they tried as best they could. But when a woman's heart is heavy, weighed down with too many thoughts, sexual release becomes nearly impossible. My mind was consumed, day and night, with the knowledge that Calira was now locked in a marriage with another. This woman of mystery had stolen what I had so desperately longed for, standing in the way of the life I had dreamed of.

I had been his whore, a secret warmth for his bed, but that was never enough for me. My reputation had already been tarnished by his father, and in my desperation, I had allowed Calira to take me, foolishly hoping that it would lead to something more. But I wanted to be more than just his whore—I wanted to be his wife, and one day, with Dovium's help, his queen. No woman in her right mind desires to be merely a rutting post, used and discarded when convenient. Even a mistress is cared for, showered with gems and gifts, her status elevated by the monarch's favor. But I was not even granted that small dignity.

Everything I had wanted, everything I had worked for, had been stolen from me, and I didn't even know the identity of the thief. I had never loved anyone the way I loved Calira. I had bared my soul to that damn dragon, revealing my deepest fears, my most cherished dreams, things I had never shared with another soul. I had trusted him with my heart, made my intentions clear from the very beginning. I never hid the fact that he was the one I wanted to spend the rest of my life with.

The thought of how he repaid that love made me sick to my stomach. Years I had spent waiting for a proposal that, deep down, I knew would never come. Perhaps it was his father's influence, or the public's disapproval of my lineage, or maybe he was simply full of shit. After all, a union between us was illegal, a violation of the laws that governed our world. But that did nothing to lessen the sting of betrayal.

And now, here I was, reduced to a lowly, broken whore, while he was poised to become king. The contrast was stark, a cruel reminder of how far I had fallen and how high he had risen. The love I had once believed in so fiercely was now a bitter memory, a painful wound that refused to heal. The future I had imagined was gone, replaced by a bleak existence where my only worth was the pleasure I could provide to men who cared nothing for me.

In the end, I was left with nothing but anger and resentment, my dreams shattered and my heart hardened. I had loved him with everything I had, but that love had brought me nothing but ruin. And as I lay in my bed, staring at the ceiling, I vowed that I would never allow myself to be used like that again. I would find a way to reclaim my life, to rise from the ashes of what had been destroyed. And when the time came, I would make sure that Calira and everyone else who had wronged me would know the full extent of the pain they had caused.

There is no greater feeling of betrayal than the one that twists deep inside a woman's soul when she realizes she's been used, led on and discarded like she was nothing. We give our hearts to these men—sometimes to women too—pouring every ounce of ourselves into the love we believe will be returned in kind. We would do anything for them—steal, lie, kill, even offer up our own lives if it meant protecting them. But after we've given everything, holding back only the breath we need to survive, they leave. They find someone else—someone younger, richer, perhaps more beautiful—and hand over the life that was meant to be ours, the life we fought and sacrificed for.

Some men, after taking what they want, leave quietly, moving on with their lives as if we never existed. Others—crueler, viler—take pleasure in rubbing their new conquest in our faces, watching us break under the weight of their betrayal. It feeds their egos, each notch on their belt making them feel like bigger men. Calira became one of those men. He was the prince, and as such, he took on the role of the breaker, the one who leaves wreckage in his wake.

He paraded his new wife through the city, showing her off like a prized possession. The crowds buzzed with excitement and chatter, their voices split between those who supported the marriage and those who, like me, turned their noses up in disdain, bitter, jaded, and seething with jealousy. The voices of the supporters rang the loudest, their praise cutting through the air like knives.

"Oh, how lovely she is! Congratulations, Lord and Lady Raye'Zore!"

"A fine couple! Look at her gown! Such fine fabric—the prince spoils his wife!"

""The new bride is so kind! She has brought alms for the poor and food for the children!"

Each word twisted in my gut like a blade, a searing reminder that it should have been me out there. I was in the kitchen, slicing potatoes, my eyes glued to the window as I watched them pass by. My hands shook with rage, and I bit down on my lower lip so hard that I tasted blood. Whoever this woman was, I wanted her gone, erased from existence. She had taken my life, the life that Calira had promised me before his father snatched it away.

The fury inside me boiled over, and I hurled the knife across the room, watching it bury itself deep into the wall with a satisfying thud. But the satisfaction was fleeting, quickly replaced by a cold, bitter resolve. Outside, a group of people gathered near my window, their voices rising as they discussed the spectacle unfolding in the streets. I cracked the glass ever so slightly, straining to hear their words, all while pretending to be absorbed in my task, grabbing another knife to keep up the charade.

Their conversations were a mix of admiration and envy, their words dripping with the same bile that churned in my own stomach. They talked of how radiant the bride looked, how generous she was, how fortunate the prince was to have found such a perfect match. But beneath their praise, I could hear the undercurrents of resentment, the same bitterness that coursed through my veins. They, like me, knew that this marriage was a farce, a cruel twist of fate that had robbed me of the future I was owed.

The knife in my hand trembled as I imagined plunging it into the heart of the woman who had stolen everything from me. I wanted her to suffer, to feel the pain that had become my constant companion. But more than that, I wanted her gone, erased from Calira's life and from mine.

As I listened to the voices outside, my anger crystallized into something harder, sharper. This wasn't over. I would find a way to reclaim what was mine, to make them all pay for the betrayal that had shattered my heart. The woman in the fine gown, with her alms and her false kindness, had taken my place. But she wouldn't hold it for long. My time would come, and when it did, I would be ready.

For now, I would wait. I would bide my time, sharpening my anger like the knife in my hand, until the day I could strike. And when that day came, the world would see just how deep a woman's betrayal could cut.

The voices outside my window were a chorus of scorn and bitterness, feeding the dark thoughts that had taken root in my heart.

"Who does this fat cow think she is?! Marrying a dragon as powerful as Prince Calira! My family is worth more than her, and we're nothing more than farmers."

I smiled to myself, savoring their contempt. They saw it too—the absurdity of this marriage, the injustice of it all. The prince had a taste, and this woman didn't fit it. She was pale and ordinary, a stark contrast to the exotic allure that Calira had always been drawn to. His preference for those with darker skin, with curls in their hair, was well known, and it was a taste that the Frostfire breed rarely indulged. The favored ones were typically those with alabaster skin and long silver hair, the traditional beauty that aligned with their cold, regal heritage. But I was none of those things. I was a forbidden fruit, something rare and enticing in a sea of the ordinary.

"Mark my words, this has something to do with war. The prince has a taste, and she ain't it. I heard that this joining was by the hand of the king himself." One man said.

My grin widened at that. The man was right. This marriage wasn't a matter of love; it was politics, a union forged not by Calira's heart but by the king's will. The idea that Calira might be trapped in a marriage he didn't want, that he could still harbor feelings for me, filled me with a twisted sense of hope. All I needed was a sign—a single thread of unhappiness in his face—and I could forgive him. I could believe that his heart still belonged to me, that this marriage was a mere formality, a cage from which he longed to be free.

"Either way, those are going to be some ugly little dragons. Look at her nose—it's flat as a pig's." Spoke another.

"Ugly little dragons? Is our new princess already with child? Or in their case, children?" Another whispered.

"Aye, look at her belly. She's pregnant indeed. With her features though, Prince Calira is in for a real surprise. Her genes are going to shoot the poor lad's good looks directly into the shitter." A woman added.

I had to stifle my laughter. Their words were like sweet poison, feeding my rage and fueling my twisted happiness. It felt good, so good, to know that I wasn't alone in my hatred. The thought of that woman carrying Calira's children, of her swollen belly full of life that should have been mine to give him, made my blood boil. But still, I needed to see him. I needed to look into his eyes and find that one ribbon of unhappiness, the proof that he still loved me, that this was all a mistake. But when I looked up, there he was, smiling from ear to fucking ear.

It wasn't the practiced, polite smile that royals wear like armor, the mask they put on for the people. No, this was genuine, a smile that reached his eyes, that lit up his whole face. He was happy—truly, deeply happy—and the sight of it felt like a knife to my gut. My hand tightened around the knife I held, the metal creaking under the force of my grip. The vision of rushing out into the crowd flashed before my eyes. I could see myself pushing past the guards, plunging the blade into her, starting with her womb.

I wanted to gut her. I wanted to see the life she carried spill out onto the cobblestones, to hear her scream as I tore away the future she had stolen from me. Once for taking my lover, and twice for daring to carry his children. My mind raced, my breath coming in ragged gasps as the rage consumed me, clouding my vision, twisting my thoughts into something feral and dark.

But then, something stopped me. It wasn't fear of the consequences or doubt in my abilities—it was the realization that killing her wouldn't change anything. Calira was happy, and nothing I did would erase that smile from his face. The woman, the marriage, the child—it was all real, and I was nothing more than a ghost from his past, a shadow that no longer had a place in his world.

The knife clattered to the floor, slipping from my trembling hand as the reality of it all crashed over me like a wave. The life I had imagined, the future I had dreamed of—it was all gone, lost to the woman who now stood at his side. And no amount of bloodshed would bring it back.

I slumped against the wall, my body shaking with silent sobs as the last of my hope crumbled to dust. The rage, the jealousy, the hatred—they were all that was left of me now. And as I sat there, broken and defeated, I realized that I had nothing left to live for. Nothing but the hollow ache of a love that had died long before this day.

And yet, deep in the pit of my despair, a seed of something darker took root. If I couldn't have him, if I couldn't destroy the life he had chosen over me, then I would find another way to make him suffer. I would become the nightmare that haunted his happiness, the shadow that lingered in the corners of his perfect life.

I would take my time, and when the moment was right, I would strike. Not with a knife, but with something far more insidious. I would unravel his world, piece by piece, until there was nothing left but the ashes of what he had once held dear. When he finally realized what he had lost, it would be too late. For him, and for her.

The thought of killing him came swiftly, like a dark whisper in my ear. If I couldn't have him, then no one should. No one could ever give him what I had—no one had nursed him back to health when he was sick, or endured his annoying habits with patience and love. No one had offered their body, mind, and heart to him on a golden platter, only to have him piss on it. I had been raped, beaten, and banished from the only home I had ever known. I had been persecuted for a murder I didn't commit, and I had been made a scapegoat for his vile, egotistical, tyrannical father.

Watching them stroll down the street, arm in arm, turned what little love I had left into pure, unadulterated hatred. And no one can hate like a Tyliquin witch. Our grudges are legendary. Hatred is one thing when it festers in the brain, but when it sinks its fangs into the heart, the venom lingers, turning us into something even the gods and demons fear. The old stories say that witches grow ugly with their malice, that they develop warts and hunchbacks, but that's a lie. No, we glow with a terrible beauty, a fire that lures the unsuspecting to their doom.

Rage was my puppet master now, pulling my strings, commanding my every move. I left my work, climbed the stairs, and pushed my way into the bustling city. Calira was only a few buildings away, his princess stopping to show her generosity at every turn. I knew what she was doing—purchasing the approval of the people. But no amount of gold could ever buy mine. I forced my way through the crowd, shoving and being shoved until, finally, I reached the front.

"Prince Calira!" I screamed, my voice cracking with the effort. I needed him to see me, to look at me with the love and passion he once had, to calm the beast that was rising within me. But my voice was drowned out by the others, all calling his name with false praise. I had to stand out, to say something that would reach him above all the noise.

"Nox'omay meihindo drakon'mey!" My dragon of night, I called out, every syllable infused with the force of my desperation, spoken in the tongue only he would recognize. It worked. He stopped and turned, his eyes searching the crowd until they found me.

I fell to my knees, bowing my head as I prayed to any god that would listen. "A moment of your time, your majesty! I beseech you!" I pleaded, hoping that he would come to me, that he would recognize the love we once shared. But, as always, the gods were deaf to my prayers. Instead of Calira's rough, familiar hand lifting my face, it was a delicate, feminine touch that raised my chin.

"You poor soul," the woman said, her voice sickeningly sweet. "Let me help you up. The crowd can be unforgiving, can it not?" I looked up into the face of the woman who would one day be queen. The citizens were right—she was ugly. At least I had that small comfort. I was far better looking than she could ever hope to be. She was one of those unfortunate souls who had to compensate for their lack of beauty with kind actions. I would rather have beauty in flesh and ugliness within than to look like her.

She helped me to my feet, her hand still resting on my arm as we spoke. "Yes, they can be," I said, forcing the words out despite the bile rising in my throat. "Perhaps you and your husband should tread these streets with caution. This city is filled with men who would love nothing more than to end the life of a monarch. Might I ask your name, your majesty?" The words nearly choked me, the reality of her title strangling my pride.

"I am Alexandria of House Oila," she said with a chuckle. "Forgive me, I suppose I am Princess Alexandria Raye'Zore now. I am sure a woman as stunning as you has a name in the likeness of your beauty."

If only she knew how much I wanted to strangle her with her own hair. I wondered if she would still be so kind then. "My name is Tonisa, your majesty," I replied, struggling to keep my voice steady.

She smiled, pressing her cheek to mine in a gesture that felt like acid on my skin. "A unique and southern name," she murmured, taking a strand of my hair in her hand, examining it with a fascination that made my skin crawl. "Your hair is so interesting! How densely it curls, how rough the strands are— amazing. Perhaps you could become my lady-in-waiting. I have always been curious about the happenings of this city. To be honest, I do not have many friends in Crystal Springs. You and I are quite alike, I believe. Neither of us were born of this land. I think we could be great companions."

Her offer was my chance, the opportunity I needed to get back into the castle, to pry Calira away from this life he seemed so content with. "I would love nothing more, your majesty," I said, forcing a smile that I hoped would mask the hatred bubbling beneath the surface. "I have served many all my life. To serve a ruler as kind and generous as yourself would be an honor."

And so, the seeds of my plan were sown. I would accept her offer, bide my time, and slowly, methodically, I would tear her world apart from the inside. I would remind Calira of what we once had, of the passion and love he had lost. And when the moment was right, I would strike, taking back what was mine, destroying anyone who stood in my way.

Calira made his way toward us, his gaze barely lingering on me before he spoke. "Come, my love, I tire of this city. Let us return home where we belong." His words were cold, dismissive, and then, as if to drive the dagger deeper, he kissed her right in front of me. It was as though I had become invisible, a ghost from his past that no longer mattered. The realization that this homely wench had replaced me hit like a punch to the gut.

Without a second glance, he placed a heavy sack of gold into my hand—payment for my silence, perhaps—and pulled his wife away from me. She followed him without question, her obedience infuriating in its simplicity. She was nothing more than a well-trained dog, doing as he commanded without a thought of her own.

"Remember my offer, Lady Tonisa. I hope you will accept it," Princess Alexandria called over her shoulder, her voice filled with a kindness that only deepened my loathing. And just as quickly as they had come, they were gone, leaving me standing there, stunned and trembling with a mix of emotions I could barely contain.

The cold indifference Calira had shown me was like a slap in the face. He had dismissed me, pushed me aside as if I were some common peasant unworthy of his attention. The realization that I had been so easily replaced made the hatred in my veins burn hotter. But even as that hatred consumed me, there was another feeling running alongside it, a feeling I couldn't shake—love. As much as I despised him in that moment, I still loved him. The need to be at his side, to reclaim what I had lost, was a pathetic yearning I couldn't rid myself of.

I clutched the sack of gold tightly, my knuckles white as I fought to keep my composure. The conflicting emotions waged war within me, tearing at my sanity. How could I still love him after everything he had done? After he had humiliated me, discarded me like I was nothing? But despite all logic, despite the pain and betrayal, I couldn't let go of the belief that he was mine and I was his.

This wasn't over. Not by a long shot. Calira had pushed me away, but I would find a way back into his life, back into his heart. The princess might have his favor now, but I would see to it that she didn't keep it for long. I would take up her offer, become her lady-in-waiting, and slowly, methodically, I would dismantle the life she had stolen from me.

The gold in my hand was heavy, a symbol of the price he had placed on my silence, but it would also be the key to my revenge. I would use it to fund my plans, to make sure that when the time came, I would be ready to reclaim what was rightfully mine. Calira might think he could forget me, but I would make sure that he never did. He would remember, and when he did, it would be too late for him to undo the damage I would wreak.

ELEVEN

Four days had passed since my encounter with Alexandria, and each day weighed heavier on my mind than the last. The thoughts swirled endlessly, questions gnawing at me, leaving me restless and uncertain. Should I really return to serve a family that had banished me, humiliated me, and left me for dead? Would I be a fool to degrade myself, to put myself back under their thumb, just to satisfy my thirst for revenge? And what if Ramsra discovered my defiance? Would he have me killed for daring to return, for refusing to stay banished as he decreed?

And then there was Alexandria herself. Could she even offer me such a position? Did she have the authority, or was it just a gesture of pity, a way to keep a potential threat close and controlled? These questions tormented me, their answers elusive, leaving me trapped in a web of doubt and anger.

The life I had now was far from perfect, but it was mine. I wasn't bound to anyone, no master to answer to, no chains to hold me down. I had the freedom to live as I chose, to make my own decisions, even if they led me down dark paths. But even with that freedom, there was an emptiness inside me, a void that had been there ever since Calira had left my side. Being with him, even in the shadows, had given me a sense of purpose, a feeling of wholeness that I hadn't been able to replicate on my own.

I knew the risks of returning to the castle, of placing myself under Alexandria's watchful eye. I would be stepping back into a world that had cast me out, into the arms of a family that had used and discarded me. But the thought of staying here, of continuing this half-life without him, was unbearable. No amount of gold or freedom could fill the emptiness that gnawed at my soul.

As much as I hated to admit it, I needed to be close to Calira. I needed to see him, to feel his presence, even if it meant playing a dangerous game. Perhaps I was a fool, driven by love and madness, but what choice did I have? The alternative was to live a life of quiet misery, haunted by what could have been, forever longing for the man who had once been mine.

But revenge... that was something else entirely. Revenge could be the salve for my wounded pride, the means to reclaim what had been taken from me. It could give me the power to control my fate once more, to turn the tables on those who had wronged me. But would that power be worth the cost of my dignity, of my soul?

Each day I spent in contemplation only deepened my uncertainty, the questions swirling like a storm in my mind. My life, my freedom, was all I had left—but what was freedom without purpose, without the one thing that had made me feel whole?

The decision weighed heavily on me. To go back would be to walk into the lion's den, to risk everything for a chance at revenge and the faint hope of reclaiming Calira's heart. To stay would be to live in quiet desperation, forever yearning for what I had lost.

In the end, it would come down to one question: what was I willing to sacrifice? My freedom, my pride, my very life? Or could I find a way to have it all—to serve Alexandria, to reclaim Calira, and to exact my revenge on those who had wronged me? The answer was as murky as the feelings that swirled within me, but one thing was clear: whatever path I chose, it would define the rest of my life.

And I knew, deep down, that I couldn't ignore the pull of that decision much longer.

I spent another week grappling with my decision, but in the end, the hunger for vengeance won out. That morning, Rose and I were in the kitchen, the scent of sizzling bacon mingling with the muffled symphony of pleasure seeping through the walls of our brothel. As we flipped pancakes and chatted about trivial things, I finally asked her to come with me. I couldn't bear the thought of venturing to the capital alone, leaving behind my one true light in this dark world.

"Rose," I began, trying to sound casual despite the urgency in my voice, "why don't you come with me? We could build a new life there, far from the grime of this place."

But Rose's hand stilled over the stove, her expression shadowed with doubt. "Tonisa," she said quietly, "I don't think it's wise for you to go back there. Not after everything that happened. Not with vengeance in your heart. You're playing with dragons, my dear, and that's a game where the loser is always the one who gets burned."

"Please, Rose," I pleaded, my voice dropping to a whisper. "Life behind those castle gates is safer than the streets we call home. You remember the raids, the fires... we barely survived. At least there, we'd have a chance."

She turned to face me fully, her eyes reflecting a sorrow deeper than I'd ever seen in them before. "And what then? Yes, our city is dangerous, but we can run, hide if we must. In the draconic court, we'd be nothing more than pawns. I'm paid for what I do here, but there? We could be taken, tortured, or worse.

The prince has you wrapped around his clawed finger, Tonisa. He'll be the death of you."

A pang of pain shot through me at her words, but I couldn't deny them. "I can't let him go, Rose. I love him. Somewhere deep inside, beneath all the chains and scales, I know he loves me too. If I can just get him away from his father's shadow… once he has his own lands, his own castle, I can reach him. I can change him."

Rose sighed, her shoulders sagging as if the weight of the world pressed down on them. "I wish you the best, sister. Truly, I do. But I can't follow you there. If anything, I'll try to build something of my own. Maybe even start my own brothel. That way, when—if—they cast you out, you'll have a place to come back to. I just hope the gods, or whoever is listening, keep you safe. The Raye'Zore clan… they're nothing but trouble."

We finished our breakfast in heavy silence, each of us lost in our thoughts. Afterward, Rose went upstairs to begin her day, while I ignored the calls of men downstairs. My mind was set. There was no turning back now.

I packed what little I had—some clothes, a few pieces of jewelry, enough food to last the journey—and left the only home I had ever known. The capital loomed on the horizon, and with it, my destiny.

Rose and I embraced as if the world itself might crumble when we let go. Words failed us both; no sentence could capture the depth of my sorrow at leaving her behind. Her eyes shimmered with unshed tears, and one final time, she begged me not to go. I wanted to soothe her, to offer some comfort, but the pull of my heart was too strong, too relentless. I had no choice but to obey its demands.

Rose was the third most important person in my life, just behind Calira and, perhaps selfishly, myself. My heart ached to return to him, to repair the bridges that had been burned. As I stared into her tear-filled eyes, I knew this might be the last time I saw her. Rose leaned in and planted a gentle kiss on my lips, a bittersweet farewell. I returned the gesture, trying to pour all the love and gratitude I felt for her into that one brief moment. With a final, tearful goodbye, I turned away, stepping into the shadowed forest, leaving behind my best friend and the city of Arobren.

The journey back to the capital seemed far longer than it had the first time. Excitement and dread coiled around me like twin serpents, tightening their grip with each step I took. For the first time in months, I found myself praying—praying for safe passage, for strength, and, most fervently, for the king's death by the time I arrived. The forest stretched endlessly before me, its ancient trees whispering secrets to the wind. I took several breaks, not just out of necessity but to marvel at the world around me. The air was thick with the scents of pine and rich earth, laced with the delicate aroma of lavender that clung to the breeze. The forest was alive, teeming with creatures and vibrant blooms, a stark contrast to the tumultuous thoughts swirling within me.

The closer I got to Crystal Springs, the more the forest seemed to swell with life. When I finally reached the gateway to the castle known as the Rise, the sun had dipped below the horizon, surrendering the world to night's embrace. Exhaustion settled into my bones, and I knew I needed to rest before facing what awaited me.

I found a small, secluded spot near a babbling stream and decided to make myself presentable. The journey had left me weary and worn, but a bath would rejuvenate me, at least in body, if not in spirit. The water was cool, a refreshing balm against the heat of the day and the weight of my thoughts. As I submerged myself, I let the water wash away the dirt and grime of the road, imagining it cleansing me of the doubts and fears that clung just as stubbornly.

The next day, I would face Calira. I would confront the demons of my past. But for that night, I allowed myself a moment of peace, floating in the cool water.

I slept deeply that night, the exhaustion from my journey overpowering the ache in my feet. When I awoke the next morning, the first sounds that greeted me were the blaring of trumpets and the steady beat of drums. The melody was unmistakable—someone of royal blood was preparing to leave the castle on a journey.

With a sense of urgency, I gathered my belongings and hurried to the edge of the Rise, eager to see who it was. As I peered through the trees, my heart nearly stopped. Ramsra, the king I had prayed would be dead, was still very much alive. But the gods had answered my prayers in part—he was leaving. By his side walked Hexonia, Calira's younger sister, her delicate form dwarfed by the imposing figure of her father. From what I could discern, this was a journey tied to marriage or the negotiation of one.

They disappeared into a grand carriage, surrounded by the king's army. Calira and Alexandria stood at the gates, waving them off before retreating back into the castle. I seized the moment, quickly making my way toward the gates, hoping to slip in unnoticed. However, the guards halted me, their eyes narrowing with suspicion. To my dismay, none of them recognized me.

"What business do you have here, girl?" one of the guards demanded, his tone laced with disdain.

"I am here at the request of Princess Alexandria," I replied, my voice steady despite the nervous flutter in my chest. "She required my services as a lady-in-waiting during her recent visit to Arobren."

The second guard, a burly man with cruel eyes, stepped forward and wrapped his fingers around my throat, squeezing just enough to cut off my air. My belongings tumbled from my grasp as I clawed at his hand, desperate for breath.

"What would Princess Alexandria want with the likes of you?" he sneered. "Dark skin, curled hair… a woman of sin by the looks of you."

I struggled to inhale, lifting my chin to gasp for air. "Those are the very reasons she found me intriguing, sir," I managed to choke out. "Please, I beg you, release me so I may fulfill her commands."

The first guard placed a hand on his companion's shoulder, urging him to relent. "Let her go. It's not our place to meddle in royal affairs. You know the princess has a penchant for inviting all manner of uncivilized creatures into these gates. Let her husband deal with it."

With a scowl, the man shoved me to the ground, his grip loosening as I collapsed into the dirt. I rubbed my bruised throat, swallowing the bitterness that rose within me. I had come with peace and respect, only to be met with scorn and abuse. As I bent to retrieve my scattered belongings, the second guard spat in my face, laughing cruelly as he yanked me back to my feet.

"Aye, I'll let her in," he said with a smirk, "but not before we search her. Can't be too careful, can we?"

His hands roamed over my body, lingering on my breasts and thighs, his touch violating and lewd. He lifted my skirts high enough for anyone watching to see beneath them, and when his filthy fingers slid between my legs, I had to fight the urge to rip out his throat. But I had no weapon, no means to defend myself, so I stood there, my head held high, enduring the humiliation for the sake of the dragon I loved.

"Quite the loose whore," he murmured, his breath rank and stomach-turning. "I bet you've got your weapons hidden up your ass. Let's have a look, shall we?"

I wrenched myself away from him, baring my teeth in a low growl. "I have no intention of harming the princess or her husband, the prince! I am here under their orders. Now let me pass, or your fun will come at a higher cost than you can afford!"

"That's enough," the first guard interjected, opening the gate. "Let her through. The last thing we need is Prince Raye'Zore's wrath raining down on us."

"Thank you," I said sharply, the words like acid on my tongue. "May you both have a joyous and forgiving day."

As I stepped through the gates, my eyes wandered over the grounds, marveling at how much had changed in my absence. The gardens were a testament to a woman's touch, the hedges trimmed into perfect shapes of the local wildlife, the ponds and fountains brimming with waterlilies. Crystalline Keep had transformed, its beauty undeniable even to one as bitter as I felt in that moment.

I approached the grand doors and knocked, the sound echoing through the still morning air. I waited, heart pounding, until at last, the doors swung open.

And there he stood—Calira, the one I valued above all else. My heart leapt at the sight of him, but the shadows in his eyes made me falter. Whatever lay ahead, I knew this reunion would be anything but simple.

TWELVE

"**T**onisa, what in the gods' name are you doing here? Tell me you were not foolish enough to accept my wife's offer." Calira's voice cut through the silence, sharp and edged with a mix of fear and anger. His usually composed face was twisted with worry, the displeasure in his eyes a stark contrast to the warmth they once held for me. The dragon I had known and loved was buried deep within the man standing before me, if he existed at all.

I searched his gaze, desperate to find a flicker of the connection we once shared, but all I saw was the cold, unyielding mask of duty. "Yes," I answered, my voice steady despite the storm brewing inside me. "I have always been foolish where you are concerned. If it means giving up my freedom to stand by your side, then so be it. Your wife seems… kind enough in her own way."

The lie tasted bitter on my tongue, but I spoke it nonetheless, hoping it might soften him, might sway him to see me as more than a burden. I knew better than to trust the dragoness, but I clung to the fragile hope that my words could bridge the chasm between us.

"You're mad," he hissed, stepping closer, his voice low and urgent. "Do you have any idea what my father would do to us if he discovered you here? You have to leave, Tonisa. I shouldn't even be speaking to you. My wife… she's blind to the true nature of our marriage, and I intend to keep it that way."

His words were a dagger to my heart, sharp and unforgiving. But beneath the harshness, I heard something else—a confession, perhaps, of the chains that bound him to a life he never chose. My heart leapt with a dangerous mix of hope and despair. Surely, he had been forced into this union, shackled by duty rather than desire.

Before I could think, I acted on pure emotion. I slammed the door shut behind me, cutting off the world outside. My belongings tumbled to the floor, forgotten, as I closed the distance between us. My fists clenched the fabric of his tunic, pulling him closer, my need for him overriding all sense of caution. Tears brimmed in my eyes, the weight of my longing dragging me down, threatening to crush me under the enormity of it all.

"Calira," I whispered, my voice trembling as I fought to keep my composure. "I cannot leave you. Not now, not ever. Whatever the risks, whatever the cost… I need you. I need us." My knees buckled, and I began to sink, the burden of my love too heavy to bear alone.

But even as I fell, I prayed that he might catch me, that somewhere deep inside, the dragon I once knew would emerge from the darkness, if only for a moment, to save us both.

"Calira… my love, my only…" My voice trembled, but I held tight to him, desperate for answers, for any sign that the man I loved was still within the cold shell before me. "Please, don't turn me away. Not now, not after everything we've endured. What has your father done to you? What horrors has he forced upon you?" My fingers dug into his blouse, as if by holding on, I could pull the truth from him. "Has he sacrificed you as he did me? Did he command you to marry that vile creature?"

My whispered words carried the weight of a thousand unspoken fears. But before I could find any solace, Calira's hands clamped down on my shoulders, his grip iron-strong as he forced me away from him. "Get a hold of yourself, woman!" he barked, his voice as sharp as the crack of a whip. "Mere moments ago, you spoke nothing but sweet lies about my wife, and now you dare accuse her? Understand this—if you stand within these walls, it is only because of her mercy."

He shook me violently, the suddenness of it forcing a gasp from my lips. "You killed my mother! The queen! Do you even comprehend the gravity of your sin? You took her life, you vile witch!"

His words struck me like a blade, each syllable slicing through the fragile remnants of my pride. My knees threatened to give way as the truth settled over me like a suffocating shroud. Tears welled in my eyes, spilling down my cheeks as my heart shattered within my chest. Ramsra had poisoned his mind, turned him against me so thoroughly that he looked at me now as if I were nothing more than a wretched beggar.

"No! No, I didn't—" I sobbed, my voice cracking under the weight of his accusation. "I loved her, Calira, and she loved me in her own way. I would never harm her, never harm you! You were all I had! Your father... he knew, he knew how much I loved you, and he wanted us apart. He wanted to erase me from your life, to keep our love from tainting your bloodline. You have to believe me!"

But even as I pleaded, I saw the doubt in his eyes, the seeds of mistrust Ramsra had planted deep within his soul. My heart ached with the knowledge that the man I loved was slipping further from my grasp, pulled away by forces I could no longer fight alone.

His anger crashed over me like a tidal wave, sending me sprawling on the cold stone floor once more. It seemed this was where I belonged now, beneath him, crushed by the weight of his fury. "You killed my mother out of your own greed," he spat, his voice laced with venom. "My love wasn't enough for you. Our secret wasn't enough. Get your things and leave, and do it quickly. If you don't, I'll throw you into a cell and let my father decide your fate when he returns."

The nausea churned violently in my stomach, and I had to fight the urge to vomit. Swallowing back the bitter bile that burned my throat, I forced myself to stand, though my legs trembled with the effort. My mind reeled with disbelief, but my heart refused to accept the cruel twist of his words. "No... no, you wouldn't do this. You came after me when I was banished. You brought me food, a horse... You still had love in your heart for me then, just as you do now."

His eyes, once filled with warmth and passion, were cold as ice as he sneered down at me. "You're mistaken, Tonisa. I came after you because my lust drove me to it, nothing more. You were a beautiful, desirable woman, and I couldn't resist the allure of taking a Tyliquin to my bed. I brought you provisions as payment, not out of love or loyalty. That's all it ever was."

His words cut deeper than any blade, each one a calculated strike meant to sever the bond between us. "I have a wife now," he continued, his tone dripping with disdain. "Such immature thoughts are beneath me. They have no place in my mind, and neither do you."

His rejection felt like a death sentence, and the world around me seemed to blur as my heart broke anew. The man before me was not the Calira I had known, the one I had loved with every fiber of my being. This was someone else, a stranger wearing the face of the man I would have given my life for.

But even as his words crushed my spirit, a small, stubborn part of me refused to believe that all the love we had shared was gone. Somewhere deep inside him, beneath the layers of anger and manipulation, I knew the Calira I loved still existed. Yet, for the first time, I feared that the man standing before me was beyond saving—that I had truly lost him to the darkness.

There it was—the grim warning Rose had given me echoing in my mind like a haunting refrain. She had been right all along; this man, this dragon, would be the death of me. His venomous words sliced through my soul, leaving me hollow. Without his affection, without his approval, I felt like nothing, as if the very essence of my being had been stripped away.

"Calira," I pleaded, my voice trembling with the desperation of a woman on the edge of despair. "You don't mean that. Those are your father's words, not yours. You're being guided by his lies, twisted by his deceit. Our love… it was always enough for me. I never needed anything more. I didn't kill your mother. Your father did."

My words seemed to land like a blow. He stepped back, his expression a mix of shock and something else, something deeper that flickered in his eyes for just a moment. For several long, excruciating seconds, he couldn't even look at me. I could see the gears turning in his mind, the war between truth and the poison his father had fed him. But then, as quickly as the moment came, it passed. His face hardened, and whatever humanity had surfaced was buried once again.

He turned on me, his eyes now filled with cold malice. Without a word, he lifted me off the ground and opened the heavy door to the castle. "Murder and lies—the true nature of a Tyliquin witch," he spat before hurling me out and slamming the door behind me with a finality that echoed through my bones.

I crumpled to the ground, tears flowing freely, each one a drop of the pain and loss that consumed me. My heart burned with a fierce, unrelenting ache, longing for him even after all that had happened. I looked around, dazed and broken. Everything I owned, everything that tied me to my past and my love, was now locked away behind that door. I sat in a heap of fabric, hiding my face in shame and despair.

The sound of galloping hooves pierced through the haze of my sorrow, and I looked up to see Rose charging toward me, her expression one of pure terror. She dismounted with urgency and rushed to my side, her arms wrapping around me in a protective embrace. I collapsed into her chest, weeping with a grief that felt bottomless.

"Tonisa! By the gods, what have they done to you?" Rose's voice was frantic as she lifted her skirt to wipe my tears, her hands trembling as she checked me for injuries.

"You were right, Rose… he wouldn't have me. He turned me away, just like his father did." I told her. My tears were like acid, burning trails down my cheeks. My eyelids felt impossibly heavy, and my body was so weak I could barely move. "What will I do now?"

"None of that matters anymore, sister," Rose said firmly, her voice laced with urgency. "We have to go. We have to leave this cursed place and get as far away as we can. Gailian soldiers have taken refuge in Arobren. I rode here as fast as I could to warn you. They have dragons with them, Tonisa. Something dangerous is brewing. You must leave Prince Raye'Zore and his brood to their own destruction and save yourself. You didn't listen to me before, but I beg you—listen to me now."

Her words cut through the fog of my despair, igniting a spark of fear that pushed through the numbness. I knew Rose was right. I had ignored her warnings before, blinded by my love for Calira, but now… now I had nothing left to hold on to. All that remained was the desperate need to survive, to escape the fate that seemed to be closing in on me from all sides.

I nodded, forcing myself to stand with Rose's help, my body trembling with the effort. "Let's go," I whispered, the words barely audible but filled with the resolve that had been buried beneath my heartache. "Let's leave this place behind and never look back."

The Gail's of Judgment. They were the keepers of balance, the enforcers of a sacred order that even dragons feared. Only they held the power to condemn and punish those magnificent beasts for their transgressions. But now, my life hung in the balance—a life that no longer seemed to matter, not when Calira's safety consumed my every thought. He had turned me away, yet that rejection only strengthened me.

"When did they arrive, Rose? How long did it take you to get here?" I forced myself to stand, though my legs trembled beneath me. My gaze shifted to the sky, then to the dense tree line that shielded the horizon.

Rose's voice was strained, her breath ragged from the relentless journey. "I got here in two days, riding nearly nonstop. The Gailian Army arrived three days ago. I would have come sooner, but slipping away without raising suspicion took a while. We don't have much time. If we leave now, we can put a generous distance between ourselves and them."

Three days. That meant the Gail's were nearly upon us. Crystalline Keep was unprepared, defenseless against such a force. But I couldn't leave—not now. "I can't go. I have to reach Calira and help him. The king and his daughter are gone. Calira can't hold this castle alone."

Rose's eyes widened, disbelief etched into her features. "Have you lost your mind?! The prince cast you aside, and now you're trying to save him? No, no! I won't let you sacrifice yourself for him again. You can't fight the Gail's—not even dragons can easily contend with them!" She grabbed my arm, pulling me toward her horse.

I wrenched free, desperation clawing at my heart. "No! This could be my chance to win him over! Run if you must, sister, but I cannot live knowing I abandoned him!" I turned back to the door, pounding on it with a fury that bordered on madness. "Prince Raye'Zore! I beseech you! The Gail's of Judgment are coming! Crystalline Keep is in grave danger!"

My fist throbbed with each strike against the iron door, bruising as my pleas fell on deaf ears. "Calira, listen to me! We must prepare! I can help you!"

Rose was beside me again, her grip tighter this time. "Tonisa, we have to go! Leave him—please!"

I fought against her hold, my body betraying my will to flee. "Rose, no! I have to help him!"

As we struggled in the courtyard, the door suddenly swung open. Calira emerged, his presence commanding, his eyes burning with an intensity that stole my breath. He reached for me, his hand closing around mine. "Get inside. Now."

But Rose, never one to cower, surged forward, striking his chest with her fists. "Let her go, you vile winged snake! You would have her give her life for yours? You are not worth such a sacrifice!"

Their argument was lost to me as Calira pulled me toward the castle. His grip was firm, yet I could sense the turmoil within him. "I will help you," I said, my voice steady despite the chaos around us. "But only if you ensure her safety as well."

He hesitated, his gaze flicking to Rose, who glared at him with unbridled contempt. "Very well," he growled. And without further argument, Calira swept us both into his arms, carrying us into the keep.

Once inside, we were met by Alexandria, her face pale with worry. She rushed to us, her hands fluttering like nervous birds. "Oh, Tonisa! You look awful—what's happened?"

Her touch ignited a flame of rage within me. Every time I saw this woman, her words found a way to wound me. But I hid my ire behind a cunning smile, one that only Rose could see. "Your Majesty, I came to answer your call, and my dear friend here has come to warn us of a grave danger. We are here to help in any way we can."

Alexandria's expression softened, her concern shifting to confusion. "What danger do you speak of?"

"The Gail's of Judgment," Rose said, her voice low and serious. "They're coming to Crystalline Keep. We don't know their purpose, but we must be ready."

Calira moved to his wife, lifting her into his arms with a tenderness that made my heart ache. "I will fight alone," he declared. "I know why they're coming, and I won't risk adding to their wrath by sending our men to battle. But I'll need another pair of eyes to guide me. As my wife, that duty falls to you."

Alexandria's eyes widened, her hands instinctively moving to her swollen belly. "I am with child, my love. I cannot risk our unborn children. Your legacy grows within me."

Calira's embrace tightened, but I could see the pain in his eyes. "I would never let anything happen to you, Alexandria. If you were to miscarry, we are young—we have time to try again. But I need you by my side, to fulfill your duty to this realm."

Alexandria stepped back, her motions clear. "I'm sorry, my love. I can't risk our children. We will find another way."

That was all the permission I needed. Her refusal had severed the last thread of my patience. Rose caught my gaze, giving me a subtle nod of approval. I stepped forward, bowing low. "Lord and

Lady Raye'Zore, if I may be so bold, there would be no greater honor than to offer my life in place of hers. I am not worth a fraction of what Princess Alexandria is. Allow me to accompany your husband into battle."

Calira turned to me, a smirk playing on his lips, though his eyes betrayed a flicker of something more—something darker. "You would give your life for a woman who does not know you? You would place yourself in the fire of battle to protect those who see you as nothing more than a hindrance? Why, Tonisa?"

I met his gaze, unflinching. "Because even when others loathe you, one life given in the stead of many is worth it. After all, the fight for freedom is what makes Evernia worth saving."

Alexandria reached me in a flurry of silken skirts and trembling hands, her lips brushing my cheeks in a cascade of fervent kisses. Her embrace was warm, desperate. "Tonisa, I owe you my life. You have my deepest gratitude. Please, bring Calira back to me safe."

I dipped into a small curtsey, my heart aching with the weight of her plea. "Of course, Your Majesty. I would throw myself in front of any bolt before I ever let it harm him."

Calira's presence loomed behind me, his voice steady despite the turmoil that churned within. "My wife, Lady Rose, you both should retire to the upper wing of the castle while Tonisa and I make our preparations."

Alexandria nodded, her eyes lingering on Calira with a mixture of love and fear. "As you command, my love."

Rose hesitated, her gaze darting to mine, silently pleading for some intervention. All I could offer was a small shrug, acknowledging the futility of her resistance. With a resigned sigh, she rolled her eyes and followed the princess up the grand staircase, leaving me alone with Calira.

I moved to his side, my hand slipping into his, a gesture of solidarity and unspoken devotion. "Together, we will defeat those who seek to harm you. I am at your side today and always."

Calira leaned down, "We must share words at length." I could feel the tension in his body, the tremor of uncertainty that rippled through him like a storm barely contained.

As he straightened, I took a moment to drink in his features, savoring the sight of him as if it might be the last. His hair, long and dark as midnight, cascaded down his back, framing the sharp lines of his jaw and the broad expanse of his shoulders. He was a warrior, a prince, and in this moment, he was mine.

THIRTEEN

The impending conversation with Calira loomed over me like a dark cloud, heavy with the weight of what was to come. I knew it would be far from easy; no amount of preparation could soften the sharp edges of our past. Years of buried truths and the relentless tide of manipulation had twisted everything between us. Undoing it all felt like trying to unravel a knotted rope soaked in darkness.

He had called for me to meet him in his chambers, just two nights after our return to the castle. I could only assume he'd been waiting for the dust to settle, for the castle to quiet its whispers, before we would face each other.

I remember the darkness of his chambers, how they seemed to close in around me like the embrace of a shadowed forest. The room was vast and foreboding, with only the fire at its heart offering any semblance of warmth. The flames roared in the hearth, casting wild, flickering light that danced across the walls and carved out his silhouette in stark relief. He stood there, an imposing figure, his power evident in every line of his form. The boy I once knew was gone, replaced by a man who had grown into something far more formidable.

As I approached him, the full extent of his transformation became clear. There was no trace of the youth I once remembered; he had become someone—something—I could only submit to. Without hesitation, I sank to my knees beside him, the folds of my gown spreading out around me like a surrendered banner. The fire's heat kissed my skin, a reminder of the danger and desire that simmered just beneath the surface.

I looked up at him, and our eyes met—his gaze inscrutable, his face a mask of cold, unyielding stone. Yet within that stillness, there was something searching, something that sought to unravel me. Was it the truth he craved? Or perhaps a lie that would make this moment easier to bear? I couldn't be certain. His beard, thick and as dark as the night itself, framed his features, drawing attention to the sharp lines of his face. He was a portrait of controlled strength, every aspect of him honed to a lethal edge.

I remained there in silence, my breath steady and measured as I waited for the prince to acknowledge my presence. This moment belonged to him, and I knew better than to break the silence first. It was his right, his power, to speak before I dared utter a word. I needed Calira to understand that I had come to him not in defiance, but in peace—a willing servant ready to face the shadows of our shared past.

In my stillness, I sought to convey my submission, to show him that I had answered his summons with an open heart, despite the heavy burden of my past choices. I was prepared to see the truth laid bare between us, no matter how it might burn. For in that truth, there was a chance for redemption—a chance to reclaim the trust that had been lost, and perhaps, to mend what had once been broken.

The warmth of his palm descended upon my head, a searing touch that penetrated even the thick curls of my hair. It was a heat unlike any other, the unmistakable warmth of a dragon concealed within the flesh of a man. There was no one else like him, no one who could command such power with a mere touch.

I fought to steady my breathing as he moved around me, his presence a force that demanded every ounce of my control. The sound of his boots echoed through the chamber, each click on the stone floor a measured, deliberate cadence. I listened intently, attuning myself to the rhythm of his steps,

allowing the steady beat to calm the wild pounding of my heart.

With every stride, he imprinted himself deeper into my mind, and I surrendered to the silence, letting the sound of his movements lull the storm within me. In his presence, I was both vulnerable and safe, caught between the fear of his power and the solace it brought.

"Tonisa," he intoned, his voice like the low rumble of distant thunder. "Either you lied to me then, or you lie to me now. Which is it? Choose your next words carefully, for if they do not ring true, any chance of my affections will vanish like smoke in the wind."

His words were a challenge, a razor-sharp blade poised to cut through whatever defenses I might still hold. This was the moment of reckoning, the moment that would determine whether I could salvage what remained between us—or lose him forever.

"I lied to you then," I confessed, my voice barely above a whisper, weighted with the gravity of my words. My head bowed low, not just in respect, but in deep regret. "I lied because I believed that in doing so, I was protecting you."

The admission hung in the air between us, a fragile thread of truth that I hoped might bridge the chasm I had created.

"Did you slaughter my mother as my father has taught me?" His question cut through the air like a dagger.

Before I could fully grasp the gravity of the moment, my head shook in response, the truth spilling out of me in a rush. "No, I never could. She was like a mother to me," I said, my voice trembling with the memory. "Your father, the king—he killed her in cold blood. I stumbled upon them, in the midst of a terrible argument. He saw me there, caught in the doorway, and he forced me to watch as he took her life."

The words tumbled out, raw and unfiltered, a confession that held all the horror and sorrow I had kept buried for so long. His hand slipped away from my head, falling to his side as he turned from me, moving toward the fire. He stood there in silence, the weight of what I had revealed bearing down on him. His head bowed, and the dark strands of his thigh-length hair cascaded forward, veiling his face from my view.

I couldn't tear my eyes away from him. The firelight flickered and danced across his body, highlighting the battle-worn scars etched into his skin, each one telling a story of survival and strength. His muscles, honed from years of training and hardship, rippled subtly with every breath he took. But it was the gleam on his skin, the way the firelight seemed to caress him, that held me captivated. He was a creature of both shadow and flame, a man forged in the crucible of darkness yet still touched by light.

"Your father is a vile and cruel man, Calira. We both know it all too well. There was a time when you feared him, and for good reason. He always made a distinction between you and your sister, never hesitating to be unspeakably cruel to you, simply because you were born different from the rest."

"My father despised me, not because I was different, Tonisa, but because I killed my brother in the nest. That's where his hatred truly began. But we are not here to discuss my past; it's yours we must confront now."

I crawled to him, the fabric of my gown trailing behind me as I clung to his leg, desperation tightening my grip. I looked up at him, my eyes wide with a longing so profound that no ocean could ever contain it.

"Tell me what you desire to know," I whispered, my voice trembling with the weight of my vulnerability. "Ask me anything, and I will give you the truth you seek."

He turned on his heel, his movements graceful yet commanding, and settled into the large chair beside me. His arms draped over the sides, the muscles in his chest on full display, each rise and fall of his breath a reminder of the strength contained within him. For a moment, he sat in silence, the harsh edges of his expression softening ever so slightly, as if he were considering something deeply. The flickering firelight played across his features, highlighting the quiet intensity in his gaze as he finally allowed a sliver of his guard to drop.

"Why would my own father kill his queen?"

"I don't know his exact reasons, Calira," I admitted, my voice steady. "I will no longer lie to you. But that night... he said something, something that haunts me still." I hesitated, choosing my next words with the utmost care. "He called her... a whore."

The word lingered in the air, a bitter echo of the cruelty I had witnessed, and I watched for any reaction in his eyes, knowing that what I had revealed could either bring us closer to the truth— or tear us further apart.

Rage flared in his eyes, dark and intense, like a storm gathering strength. His hands clenched into fists, the knuckles white with the force of his anger. I could even hear the subtle creak of leather as his toes curled within his boots. When he spoke, his voice was a low growl, barely restrained, each word vibrating with fury.

"My mother was no whore!" he spat, the sheer force of his denial reverberating through the room like the crack of a whip.

"No Calira, she was not. I would never speak the words but Ramsra would and did. That is what he said the moment before he saw a dagger into her chest."

I tried my best to remember that evening, to force myself to remember it as hard as it was. In doing so to help heal Calira I would have to face the skeletons in my own closet. My eyes brimmed with tears as my next words choked out through sobs.

"When he had finished taking your mother's life, he turned his cruelty upon me," I whispered, my voice trembling with the weight of the memory. "He raped me, Calira. That is why I did not bleed for you on the night you came to me. He stole my innocence in a bed still stained with your mother's blood. And then, to hide his wickedness, he had me banished for his own crimes."

Tears welled in my eyes, but I held his gaze, determined that he see the truth in my words. Speaking life into that dreadful night felt as though a piece of my soul was being torn from my chest. The pain was visceral, a wound that had never truly healed, now laid bare. I had never wanted Calira to know that his own father had defiled me, that he had shared in my suffering in the most vile way. But if I truly wanted to keep Calira—if I wanted any hope of a future with him—I knew that everything had to be revealed, no matter how excruciating. There could be no more secrets between us, no more shadows lurking in the corners of our love.

He rose from the chair with a suddenness that startled me, then dropped to his knees as if the weight of my truth had struck him down. The pain etched across his face mirrored the agony I had carried for so long. Without hesitation, he closed the distance between us, pulling me into his arms. I collapsed into his embrace, the strength of his hold the only thing keeping me from shattering completely.

For the first time, I allowed myself to weep against his chest, releasing the years of torment and suffering I had buried deep within. His warmth surrounded me, a balm to the wounds I had thought would never heal. But even as I clung to him, there was a shadow still lingering, a secret gnawing at the edges of my newfound solace—the secret of the child.

It was a truth too heavy, too dangerous to reveal, especially in this fragile moment when I had finally found refuge in the arms of the man I had once loved. So, I held it back, burying it deep within me, choosing instead to savor this fleeting moment of peace, of reunion, of love long denied.

His words—"Tonisa, I am so sorry"—shattered the last of my resolve. The apology, spoken with such raw sincerity, as if he bore the weight of his father's sins himself, broke me in a way I hadn't known I could break. I let go, surrendering completely to the moment, my full weight collapsing into his embrace. A wail tore from my throat, a primal scream that echoed through the chamber, releasing years of pent-up anguish. I knew no one could hear me, and for that brief, cathartic moment, I didn't care. I needed to let it all out, to purge the darkness that had haunted me for so long.

When the storm of my sorrow finally subsided, I lifted my tear-streaked face to his, and everything else ceased to exist. The world of Ramsra, with all its pain and politics, faded into nothingness. There was no past, no future—only him. His eyes held mine, and in that gaze, I found something I thought I had lost forever. The rest of the world fell away, leaving just the two of us, bound together in a moment of pure, undeniable truth. Nothing else mattered but the man before me, the man who, despite everything, still held me as if I were the most precious thing in the world.

FOURTEEN

The first light of dawn filtered through the curtains, casting a soft glow across the room. As I stirred, I found myself enveloped in the warmth of his bed, cocooned in a sense of safety that had eluded me for far too long. The steady rhythm of his breathing beside me was a gentle reminder of the night we had spent together—not in passion, but in something far more intimate.

His presence had been a balm to my weary soul, a quiet companionship that soothed the edges of my frayed nerves. Though we hadn't crossed that final threshold, the bond we'd forged felt deep, like a whispered promise of something more.

I reached out, lightly brushing my fingers against his shoulder. His skin was warm beneath my touch, and the simple act of waking him felt like a sacred ritual. His eyes fluttered open, still hazy with sleep, and I couldn't help the small smile that curved my lips.

"We need to talk," I whispered, my voice gentle yet laced with urgency. There were questions that needed answers, mysteries that had begun to unravel in the night. The Gails of Judgment were not to be trifled with, and their interest in him, in this place, troubled me more than I cared to admit.

As he slowly sat up, the lines of concern that had marred my thoughts began to fade, replaced by a renewed sense of determination. Together, we would face whatever storm was brewing. And perhaps, in the midst of it all, we would discover what it truly meant to be safe—both in each other's arms and in this perilous world.

His voice was a soft caress, laced with a tenderness that made my heart flutter. "What do you want to talk about?" he asked, his fingers gently brushing against my skin as he tucked a stray tuft of hair behind my ear. The simple gesture sent a shiver down my spine, awakening the dormant connection between us— a connection that had once felt unbreakable.

It was the touch of my dragon, the one I had yearned for, the one I had feared I would never feel again. The familiarity of it stirred something deep within me, something that had lain dormant for far too long.

I hesitated, letting the silence stretch between us as I searched his face. My gaze locked onto his eyes, those deep, molten pools of gold that shimmered with an otherworldly intensity. They were so human, yet there was an ancient, primal force lurking just beneath the surface. His eyes were a window into a soul that was both man and beast, a soul that held secrets I was desperate to uncover.

I found myself lost in them, as if those golden depths could pull me into a world where time stood still and nothing else mattered. There was a raw power in his gaze, something hidden yet undeniable, and it called to me like a siren's song. I wanted to unravel the mystery of him, to understand the force that bound us together, even as it threatened to tear us apart.

But there was more at stake than just our rekindled bond. The Gails of Judgment loomed over us, their intentions as mysterious as the man before me. I took a deep breath, gathering my thoughts, and finally spoke, my voice tinged with the gravity of what lay ahead.

"We need to talk about the Gails," I said, my eyes never leaving his. "And why they've taken such an interest in you... in us."

He shifted beside me, the bed creaking softly as he sat up against the pillows. His arms crossed over his broad chest, the muscles tensing as if bracing for the weight of the words he was about to speak. I could see the tension in his posture, the way his head dipped low, shadowing his face from my view.

When he finally spoke, his voice was clipped, almost resigned, as though the truth he carried was a burden too heavy to bear. "They are coming because of my father," he began, each word laced with a bitterness that pierced through the air between us. "In the time you were away, he has committed heinous crimes—acts so dark and unforgivable that they've summoned the wrath of the Gails. Now, those sins have fallen to me to atone for, to settle in his stead."

Calira's tone was curt, almost cold, as if distancing himself from the gravity of what he was saying would somehow make it less real. But I could see the pain etched into the lines of his face, the way his shoulders seemed to sag under the invisible weight of his father's legacy.

My heart ached at the thought of him carrying this burden alone, of the darkness that had tainted his life while I had been away. There was so much I didn't know, so much that had changed in the time we had been apart. But one thing was clear—whatever lay ahead, we would face it together.

I reached out, placing my hand gently on his arm, feeling the tension thrumming beneath his skin. "You don't have to do this alone," I whispered. "We'll face whatever comes, together."

His voice was stern, the words a clear warning. "It is not your fight." But I refused to let the distance he tried to create between us grow any wider. I moved closer, my body finding its place atop his lap, straddling him with a familiarity that neither of us had forgotten. My hands slid up into his hair, fingers threading through the soft strands as I gently massaged his scalp. The tension in his body seemed to ease under my touch, but I wasn't done.

I lifted his head, guiding him to meet my gaze, ensuring that he could see the determination burning in my eyes. Our faces were so close now, breaths mingling, and I spoke with all the love and passion that had been building within me.

"Your fights are my fights. Your sorrow is mine to share," I whispered, each word a vow, a promise etched into the very fabric of my being. "I don't support you because I have to. I support you because I want to, because I love you. And I will always love you, until my last breath."

His eyes, those deep golden orbs that had held me captive so many times before, softened at my words. I could see the conflict warring within him—the desire to protect me battling against the part of him that longed to accept the comfort I offered.

"I am here with you," I continued, my voice unwavering. "Whatever darkness your father has brought into this world, we will face it together. But I need to know, Calira. What has he done? What is it that we must prepare for?"

I watched as the walls he had built around himself began to crumble, the weight of his burdens slowly lifting, if only just enough to let me in. And in that moment, I knew—no matter the battles ahead, no matter the shadows that loomed—we would stand side by side, unbreakable.

"Ramsra... he..." Calira's voice faltered, the weight of his confession hanging heavy in the air. "He murdered an innocent," he finally continued, his words filled with a pain so raw it seemed to tear at the very fabric of the room. "But such things can never be brought to light."

The gravity of what he was telling me sent a shiver down my spine, and I felt the world shift beneath us. The man I loved was bearing the sins of his father, sins that were too dark, too damning to ever see the light of day. My heart ached for him, for the burden he carried.

"That's why... when you arrived," he went on, his voice growing quieter, as if speaking the truth aloud would make it more real, "he and my sister, Hexonia, were leaving. She is to marry the dragon who was betrothed to the one he murdered in cold blood."

The pieces of the puzzle began to fall into place, each one more twisted and tragic than the last. The departure I had witnessed wasn't just a retreat—it was a desperate attempt to cover up a crime that could tear their world apart. And yet, even in the midst of this darkness, Calira had found something that gave him hope, something that reignited the fire in his soul.

"It's why I know," he continued, his voice growing stronger, more certain, "that everything you've said to me this past evening is true. It's why I will fight for our love once more."

His words struck deep, resonating in the quiet corners of my heart. Despite the storm that raged around us, despite the sins of the past, he was choosing to fight for us. For love. For the future we could still have, even if it meant facing the shadows together.

I tightened my grip on him, pulling him closer, our foreheads touching as I whispered, "Then we will fight. We will face whatever comes, and we will do it together. Your battles are mine now, Calira, and nothing—not even the darkness of your father's deeds—will tear us apart."

His arms enveloped me, pulling me closer until there was no space left between us. I felt the warmth of his breath as he inhaled deeply, savoring my scent as if it was the air he needed to survive. His lips began to trace a path up my neck, leaving a trail of fire in their wake, and then down across my chest, each kiss igniting a spark that made me squirm beneath his touch.

The heat between us was undeniable, a force of nature that neither of us could resist. I felt the growing warmth between my thighs, a response to the hardening desire I could feel pressing against me. The sensation was intoxicating, a heady mix of lust and love that made my breath catch in my throat.

"I want you, Tonisa," he murmured, his voice rough with desire as his hands roamed possessively over my body. "I want you here and now, in my chamber, where anyone could find us together." His words were a dark, thrilling promise, one that sent a shiver of anticipation down my spine. The thought of being discovered, of letting the world see what we were to each other, only heightened the intensity of the moment.

"I want them to know that I love you," he continued, his voice growing more fervent with each word. "To see that together, we intend to claim not only the throne but the heavens themselves."

There was something fierce in his declaration, something that went beyond the physical. It was a promise of power, of unity, of a love so consuming that it could change the very course of our world. And as I looked into his eyes, I knew that this moment, this union, was more than just a joining of bodies—it was the forging of a bond that could withstand any storm, conquer any enemy.

I leaned in, pressing my lips to his, tasting the passion that simmered just beneath the surface. My hands slid down his back, pulling him closer still, until I could feel the full length of him against me, hard and ready. The world outside the chamber ceased to exist; all that mattered was this, us, and the love that burned between us like a wildfire, unstoppable and eternal.

"Then take me," I whispered against his lips, the words a challenge, a plea, and a vow all at once. "Let them see, let them know. Together, we will reign over all, and nothing will stand in our way."

It was then that he entered me, a gasp escaping my lips as the sensation of him filling me completely took hold. His long nails dug into the flesh of my back, the sharpness of them a contrast to the heat that surged between us. The girth of him stretched me in a way that was both intense and deeply satisfying, a perfect blend of pleasure and pain that made my breath hitch in my throat.

I began to move, slowly at first, savoring the way our bodies melded together, each thrust bringing us closer to that blissful union. His moans, low and guttural, spurred me on, urging me to quicken my pace, to give him the pleasure he so desperately sought. With each roll of my hips, I felt him deeper, felt the connection between us solidify into something unbreakable.

His hands traveled down to my hips, his claws gripping my skin with a possessive intensity that sent shivers down my spine. He laid back, his golden eyes fixed on me, watching as I rode him with a fervor that matched his own. There was something primal in his gaze, a hunger that matched my own as we moved together, bodies entwined in a rhythm as old as time.

The room around us seemed to fade, the world outside forgotten in the heat of our passion. All that mattered was this— this moment of pure, unfiltered connection where nothing else existed but the two of us, locked in a dance of pleasure and power. His hands tightened their grip on my hips, guiding me, urging me to move faster, harder, until the pleasure building inside of us threatened to consume everything in its wake.

I threw my head back, losing myself in the sensation, in the way our bodies fit together so perfectly, in the way his moans blended with mine to create a symphony of desire. The power I felt, the power we shared, was intoxicating, a heady mix of love and lust that made me feel invincible.

And in that moment, as I moved atop him, driving us both toward the peak of pleasure, I knew that this was more than just an act of physical union. It was a declaration, a promise that no matter what challenges lay ahead, he was mine and I his.

His thumb found its way to that most sacred part of me, the delicate bead of pleasure that sent waves of heat rippling through my body with every soft, circular motion. The sensation was electric, a sweet torment that made my breath catch and my movements falter for just a moment before I found my rhythm again. His other hand slid up to my breast, fingers squeezing with just the right amount of pressure, sending another jolt of pleasure coursing through me.

"Tonisa…" he panted beneath me, his voice thick with desire and need. The way he said my name, filled with such raw emotion, made my heart skip a beat, even as I continued to move atop him.

Every touch, every stroke of his thumb against my most sensitive spot, every squeeze of his hand on my breast, was a reminder of how deeply connected we were, how perfectly we fit together in this moment. The pleasure was building, a tidal wave of sensation that threatened to sweep us both away, and I could see the same intensity mirrored in his eyes as he watched me, his gaze locked on mine.

The room around us seemed to pulse with the energy of our joining, the air thick with the scent of our passion. I could feel the tension coiling in my belly, tightening with every thrust, every brush of his thumb against me. His moans grew louder, more urgent, spurring me on to move faster, to take us both to the edge and beyond.

My own breath was coming in ragged gasps, the pleasure nearly overwhelming as I rode him, our bodies moving together in perfect harmony. The pressure was building, spiraling higher and higher, until it was all I could do to hold on, to keep moving, to keep driving us both toward that inevitable, glorious release.

"Calira..." I moaned, my voice trembling with the intensity of the moment, the sound of his name on my lips a plea, a prayer, as the pleasure surged through me, unstoppable and all-consuming.

The climax hit me like a tidal wave, crashing over me with such force that my entire body trembled. My legs quivered, toes curling in sheer ecstasy as the pleasure rolled through me in powerful waves. My eyes fluttered, rolling back as I was consumed by the intensity of it all, every nerve ending alive and buzzing with sensation.

But just as I thought we were done, that the fire between us had finally burned out, he surprised me. With a sudden, fierce strength, he hoisted me up off the bed, his movements so quick and forceful that I barely had time to catch my breath. Before I could fully process what was happening, he slammed me into the nearby wall, the impact leaving me breathless in the most delicious way.

One of his hands pinned my arms above my head, the other wrapping firmly around my waist to hold me in place. I was utterly at his mercy, suspended between the wall and his body, and the power of the moment sent a new thrill coursing through me.

"I am not finished with you yet, my love," he growled, his voice low and filled with a fierce determination. There was a wicked smirk on his lips, a promise of what was yet to come, and I could feel my heart race in anticipation.

He kissed me then, a passionate, demanding kiss that stole what little breath I had left. His lips were insistent, his tongue claiming mine with a hunger that only fueled the fire between us. And then, without warning, he thrust into me once more, his body driving home with a force that left no room for doubt—this was not just a physical act; this was a claiming, a reaffirmation of the bond we shared.

Each powerful thrust was aimed at the very center of my soul, connecting us in a way that went beyond the physical. I could feel him everywhere, his presence overwhelming, his desire wrapping around me like a cocoon. The wall at my back only

intensified the sensation, every movement sending sparks of pleasure through my already sensitive body.

I moaned into his mouth, the sound swallowed by our kiss as he drove deeper, harder, his pace unrelenting. The world around us faded to nothing, leaving only the two of us, locked in this dance of passion and power. His grip on me tightened, his control absolute, and yet there was a tenderness beneath the roughness, a love that shone through even in the midst of our fervor.

With every thrust, he took me higher, pulling me back to the edge of ecstasy and beyond. I could feel the pleasure building again, a new wave rising to meet me, and I knew that this time, when it hit, it would be even more powerful, even more consuming than before.

And as I felt that wave cresting, as my body responded to his with an intensity that left me breathless. I felt the tension building in him, the undeniable surge of his release approaching, as his manhood swelled within me, growing harder and more insistent with each powerful thrust. His lips tore away from mine, and in a primal, breathtaking display of his true nature, he claimed me as only a dragon could.

His teeth sank into the tender flesh of my neck, a possessive bite that held me firmly in place, pinning me down so that I was completely at his mercy. The sensation was a mix of pain and pleasure, a raw, electrifying reminder of the beast that lurked within him, the powerful dragon who had chosen me as his own.

With one final, forceful thrust, he drove deeper into me than ever before, a depth that seemed to reach my very soul. The sound that escaped him was a roar of pure, unrestrained pleasure, echoing through the chamber and reverberating within me. His arm, no longer wrapped around my waist, moved to the wall beside us, and with a fierce grip, his claws dug into the stone, crumbling it beneath his strength as he reached the peak of his climax.

I could feel the full force of his release, the way his body tensed and shuddered as he gave himself over to the pleasure, and it sent me spiraling into another wave of ecstasy. The world blurred around us, nothing existing outside of this moment, this connection that bound us together so completely.

As his climax subsided, he released his bite, his lips brushing over the mark he'd left on my neck in a gesture that was both possessive and tender. His grip on the wall loosened, the stone crumbling away as he pulled me away from it, his arms wrapping around me once more.

We sank to the floor together, our bodies still trembling from the intensity of what we'd just shared. The cool stone beneath us was a stark contrast to the heat that still radiated between us, our skin slick with sweat and our chests heaving as we struggled to catch our breath.

In the quiet aftermath, with our hearts pounding in unison, I felt a deep sense of contentment, a fulfillment that went beyond the physical. We were more than just lovers now; we were bound by something far stronger, something that could never be broken.

FIFTEEN

T hey arrived with the ominous stillness of a brewing tempest, a silence so profound it resonated louder than the fiercest roll of thunder. The air itself seemed to hold its breath in anticipation, as if the world recognized the gravity of their presence. Their approach was unsettlingly graceful, as though they were specters gliding effortlessly upon the winds, their feet scarcely touching the ground. The very soil beneath them seemed reluctant to acknowledge their existence.

Their presence was a force that could not be ignored, an unspoken command that seized every gaze, stole every breath, and demanded a reverence born of equal parts awe and dread. These were no ordinary visitors; they were the Gales of Judgment, a name whispered in fearful reverence across the lands, a power so formidable that even the mightiest of dragons would tremble at their mere mention. And now, they stood before my lord, my love, their gaze heavy with the weight of a doom so absolute that I would not have wished it upon even my most bitter foe.

Calira sat upon the throne beside his wife, his regal demeanor unshaken, though I could sense the tension coiled within him like a serpent ready to strike. Rose and I sat among the courtiers, our positions close yet distant enough to remain inconspicuous. The court was bathed in an uneasy silence, every soul present holding their breath as the Gales prepared to speak.

Among them, one face stood out—a face that had haunted my dreams, the face of a warrior I had once seen on a night that felt like a lifetime ago. His emerald hair caught the dim light of the chamber, casting a surreal glow that only heightened my anxiety. I bowed my head, praying that he would not recognize me, that the past would not reach out with its cold, grasping fingers to snatch me back into its clutches.

But even as I averted my gaze, I felt the burn of his eyes upon me, a heat that crawled across the back of my neck like a flame, threatening to ignite the turmoil within me. My stomach twisted in knots, and a shiver ran down my spine at the thought of those piercing eyes locking onto mine. What would he see if he recognized me? Would he see the woman I had become, or the girl he had known in those dark, forgotten nights?

The tension in the room floated around, a living, breathing entity that fed on our fear and uncertainty. We all waited, hearts pounding, for the words that would seal our fate, knowing that nothing would ever be the same after that day.

"Your father, King Ramsra Raye'zore, has been accused of parricide," the eldest man intoned, his voice a slow, grating rasp that seemed to claw its way through the tense air of the court. His words landed like stones in the silence, and the shock of the accusation sent a collective shudder through those gathered. I could feel it reverberate through the chamber, an unspoken wave of disbelief and horror that lingered in every corner of the room.

The man who had spoken was ancient, his face etched deeply with the passage of time, every wrinkle carved into his skin like the lines of a withered map. His eyes, cold and devoid of warmth, flicked between the gathered nobles with a disdain that radiated from his very being. His mouth was perpetually twisted into a scowl, as though the weight of the world had soured every joy he might have once known.

I couldn't tear my gaze away from his hands, though. They were skeletal, long and gnarled fingers that seemed to tremble with age yet held a strange, sinister energy. His nails, jagged and cracked, were caked with grime—years of filth that had accumulated beneath them. I swallowed hard, my stomach turning with disgust as the image seared itself into my mind. This man, this decrepit figure, was the one to bring forth such a grave charge? It felt as though the foulness of his appearance somehow poisoned the very accusation he made, tainting it with malice.

He sat at the head of the group of four, his presence demanding attention despite the other figures around him. Each one was grim-faced, somber in their silent support of the words that had been spoken, but none as unsettling as the man at the center. And there, standing to his right, was a face I had not expected to see again—the copper-skinned warrior who had once darkened the doors of my old whorehouse. His bearing was as confident as ever, his sharp eyes gleaming with a mixture of intrigue and calculation, and I could feel my heart stutter at the sight of him.

Memories of that time, of the life I had worked so hard to leave behind, surged to the surface unbidden, threatening to drag me under. That warrior had been a shadow in those days, his presence always a quiet menace, and now here he was again, somehow entwined with this awful moment. I glanced at him from beneath my lashes, hoping he had forgotten me, just another face from a world he had surely long since discarded. But still, the fear lingered like a bitter taste in my mouth.

The court remained deathly still as the eldest man continued to speak, his words slowly spinning a web of accusation and suspicion that crept over us all. And yet, amidst the tension, my thoughts kept drifting back to the copper warrior and the danger he represented—a danger far more personal and immediate than even the damning accusation of parricide.

"These accusations are false, Grand Carsonal," Calira declared, his voice cutting through the tension with the sharpness of a blade. Every eye in the court turned to him, drawn to the authority he wielded with such effortless grace. He sat tall upon the throne, his gaze unwavering as it settled on the crumbling figure of the Grand Carsonal. The title might have meant power once, but in this moment, it was clear who commanded the room.

"In fact," Calira continued, his tone edged with a quiet confidence, "they are nothing more than trumped-up charges born of envy and bitterness—whispers from those who regret their failure to marry my sister, the young maiden Hexonia." His words rang out like a challenge, a thinly veiled accusation of deceit wrapped in regal restraint. A murmur rippled through the court, the name Hexonia igniting a spark of curiosity among the gathered nobles. They knew of her beauty, her grace, and the suitors who had vied for her hand—and how those suitors had been spurned.

Calira's gaze, however, did not linger on the crowd. It locked instead on the green-haired warrior, the one whose presence had set my heart racing and filled me with a dread I could scarcely conceal. The warrior stood across the chamber, his broad frame tense, a snarl curling at his lips as he met Calira's defiant stare. His eyes were like molten emeralds, simmering with barely contained fury, and his expression twisted into something dangerous. The growl that rumbled in his throat was low and menacing, the sound of a beast on the verge of unleashing its wrath.

The tension between them crackled in the air like the calm before a storm, each man sizing the other up, though the warrior was far less subtle. His grimace deepened, the muscles in his jaw working as though he was chewing over a bitter defeat, unable to stomach the truth laid bare before the court. His fists clenched at his sides, and I could see the tremor of restraint that kept him from leaping forward in protest.

But Calira did not waver. His composure remained ironclad, his expression unreadable, though there was a fire in his eyes that dared the warrior to step out of line. It was a battle of wills, and in the midst of it, I could feel the air grow heavy with the weight of unspoken history between them. There was more to this confrontation than the mere matter of parricide. There were old wounds here, scars that ran deeper than the accusations now laid bare before the court.

I shifted in my seat, the unease in my chest tightening with every heartbeat. The green-haired warrior's gaze flicked toward me briefly, a flash of recognition in his eyes. My pulse quickened. I ducked my head, feigning disinterest, but it was too late. The storm I had feared was already brewing, and I was caught in the eye of it.

As the court held its breath, waiting to see if the warrior would lash out or retreat, I knew one thing for certain—this was far from over. Whatever had begun here would not be resolved with words alone, and the green-haired warrior, driven by his hatred and perhaps something more, was not a man who would let a slight go unanswered.

"That is a lie!" the green-haired warrior bellowed, his voice reverberating off the marble walls as he stepped forward, his fury unchained. He pointed a finger squarely at Calira, the accusation hanging in the air like a blade poised to strike. The court erupted into a murmur, nobles exchanging glances, some shocked, others intrigued, as they shifted uncomfortably in their seats.

The warrior's eyes burned with a venomous intensity, every muscle in his body taut with rage as he faced not only Calira but the entire lineage that sat behind him. He stood tall and unyielding before the Grand Carsonal, who seemed almost to shrink in his seat at the force of the warrior's outburst. The ancient man watched silently, his grim face as still as stone, allowing the scene to unfold without interruption.

"Your father killed Lady Desta in cold blood," the warrior snarled, his words laced with venom. His gaze bore into Calira with an intensity that left the room thick with tension. "He murdered her to seize power—a throne and an allegiance that were never meant for him. And he did it so your sister Hexonia could be married off to Laxrindren Tay'lynn, binding her in a political union that would make your family nearly untouchable. The alliance was crafted to grant you all immunity from the judgment of the Gails through a web of deceit and power-hungry ambition!"

The air seemed to grow colder at his words, and an audible gasp echoed from the court. The name of Lady Desta, once spoken with reverence and sorrow, now carried the weight of betrayal and bloodshed. Whispers flitted through the crowd, spreading like wildfire as eyes darted toward Calira and his family, searching for cracks in the carefully maintained façade.

Calira's expression remained calm, but there was a flicker of something in his eyes, a brief moment where the mask slipped. His jaw tightened, and though he maintained his poised composure, the warrior's accusation had struck deeper than he would ever let show.

The green-haired warrior took another step forward, his presence a looming threat, his voice trembling with conviction. "Your father sacrificed the blood of an innocent dragoness to satisfy his ambition, and now you all hide behind

lies and alliances forged through murder. But not everyone has forgotten. Some of us still seek justice—real justice, not the mockery of it you've hidden behind for so long."

The court grew silent once more, the weight of the warrior's words settling over everyone like a heavy fog. His raw hatred and passion seemed to fill the space between them, his truth cutting through the formality and pretenses of the proceedings. He stood like a figure of vengeance, determined to drag every last secret into the light.

For a moment, it seemed as though the air around Calira and the warrior crackled with unspoken conflict, a collision of power and defiance. But Calira, ever the master of control, did not falter. He rose slowly from his throne, his gaze locking onto the warrior's with a deadly calm.

"You speak of justice," Calira said, his voice smooth but cold, "but what justice is there in spreading slander to serve your own bitter heart? You come into this court with accusations, with lies spun from ancient grudges, all to stir dissent. But the truth is not yours to twist Nefarious of Aga'nasta. My father's hands remain unbloodied and your heart remains scorned. All present know of your obsession with my sister."

The warrior's face twisted with fury, but Calira remained unfazed, his voice unyielding as he continued. "The alliances my father made, the decisions of this kingdom, were forged in necessity to preserve not just our rule but the peace of the realm. You accuse us of betrayal, of murder, but where were you when the kingdom stood on the edge of ruin, when only those alliances could keep us from the devastation that would have followed? You claim to seek justice—perhaps you simply seek revenge."

Silence fell again, heavy and oppressive, as the two men stared each other down, locked in a battle of wills. The entire court seemed frozen, waiting to see which way the scales would tip, and I, hidden in the sidelines, could feel the tremors of the storm growing more dangerous by the moment. The green-haired warrior was not one to back down, and Calira, as ever, would not yield an inch.

Nefarious closed the distance between them in a flash, his every step deliberate and lethal. His eyes, cold and unrelenting, locked onto Calira's with a sharpness that seemed to cut through the space. When he spoke, his voice was low, a growl simmering beneath his words, his face now mere inches from Calira's.

"I challenge you, Calira Raye'zore, to a duel," Nefarious declared, the words leaving his lips like a sentence handed down from the gods. The court gasped, shock rippling through the crowd like a wave as they watched the confrontation unfold. It was as if time itself held its breath, waiting to see what Calira would do.

For a heartbeat, Calira remained seated, his expression unreadable. But then, slowly and with the grace of a lion rising to face a rival, he stood from the throne. His regal composure didn't falter as he straightened to his full height, though his eyes glinted with something dangerous—something primal that stirred beneath his otherwise calm surface. With a single step, he closed the space between them, pushing back against Nefarious until they stood toe to toe, the tension between them almost suffocating.

"To the death?" Calira's voice was quiet, but it held a lethal weight that filled the chamber. His words were like steel, cold and sharp, and they hung in the air as if daring Nefarious to speak the fatal agreement.

My heart leapt into my throat, pounding so fiercely I was sure it would betray me. The room seemed to close in around me, the air too thick to breathe as dread coiled in my chest. I glanced at Rose, her face pale and eyes wide with the same fear that gripped me. We exchanged a single, frantic look and without words, we prayed together—prayed that Nefarious would not take that final step into a duel of death.

For a brief moment, the court was still. Even the torches seemed to flicker in anticipation as Nefarious held Calira's gaze, neither man willing to look away. Finally, the green-haired warrior spoke, his voice steady and resolute, though laced with that same unyielding fury.

"We fight until one submits," he said, his words calm yet seething with purpose. "This duel will not resolve the accusations I've brought before you today, but I will fight for my honor and the honor of my clan. You've spoken boldly, Calira, for one so protected by power and title. Let us see if you can back up your words with fang, talon, and flight."

The warrior's declaration rang through the hall, carrying the weight of generations of warriors before him—men and women who had fought with everything they had to protect their kin, their honor. The intensity of his words settled like a heavy cloak over the room, thick with the promise of violence to come.

I could feel the pulse of the crowd shift, their excitement and fear a palpable thing in the air. This would not be an ordinary duel—it was something far more dangerous. It was a clash of legacies, of old bloodlines and bitter histories that could not be erased with words alone.

Calira did not flinch. His lips curved into the barest hint of a smile, one that did not reach his eyes. He stepped back just enough to give them both space, his movements deliberate and measured. "Then so be it, Nefarious. I will honor your challenge, and we will see which of us truly stands upon the foundations of strength and valor."

My breath hitched as I watched the two men prepare, both unwilling to retreat from the path they had set upon. Whatever blood might spill in this duel, it would only be the beginning of something far greater—a battle for honor, for power, and for the truth that neither side could afford to lose.

SIXTEEN

The challenge day had been set for three days after the Gails made their fateful appearance at court, their arrival heralding the storm that now loomed over us all. Nefarious, ever eager for bloodshed, seemed to relish the thought of standing opposite Calira in battle. His desire to fight, his thirst for victory, burned visibly in his every movement, as if each passing hour only stoked the fires of his rage. And though no words had been spoken directly, it was painfully clear that Calira had struck a nerve. The mention of Hexonia—the woman who haunted the warrior's heart—had touched something deep within Nefarious, something raw and unhealed.

The tension in the castle grew with each day leading up to the duel. Whispers of the coming fight spread like wildfire, and while most of the court prepared for the spectacle with eager anticipation, I carried my fear like a stone in my chest. Calira, ever calm, ever poised, showed no sign of the worry that gnawed at me. He moved with the same quiet dignity, offering no outward hint that the duel weighed on his mind. But I knew him too well—I could see the subtle tension in his shoulders, the way his eyes lingered just a little longer on the horizon as if already planning his every move against Nefarious.

In those days before the fight, I cherished every stolen moment we had together. When the castle fell silent and the halls emptied of its courtiers and gossip, Calira and I would find refuge in the quiet places, away from the prying eyes of those who buzzed with the excitement of the coming duel. His hand in mine, we would walk through the gardens or sit by the flickering fire in his chambers, speaking in low voices about everything but the duel that loomed ahead.

I wanted him to feel my faith, to know without question that I believed in his strength, in his victory. Yet, beneath it all, a quiet terror lurked in the shadows of my thoughts. Nefarious was said to be the larger of the two, his body hardened from years of battle, his reputation built on a lifetime of fierce victories. Word had it that he was relentless in combat, a warrior born and bred with the kind of savage experience that only years of warfare could bring. And while Calira was strong, clever, and skilled with both blade and strategy, doubt gnawed at me like a persistent whisper in the back of my mind.

Still, I refused to let my fear show. Every time we were together, I smiled, I laughed, I reassured him of my faith. I kissed him with a fierce passion that belied my anxiety, hoping he could feel how much I needed him to win, not just for his honor but for the life we had begun to build together. I told him he was everything—my love, my heart, my future—and in those quiet moments, I tried to push aside the haunting image of Nefarious standing over him, victorious.

"You'll best him," I whispered one night, as we lay together in the soft glow of the dying embers. "You've faced worse than him before, and this will be no different."

Calira smiled at me, his hand gently tracing the curve of my face. "I will win," he said, his voice steady and sure. "For you, for my family, and for our future." But even as he spoke the words, I could see a flicker of something deeper in his eyes—something that told me he understood the risk, just as I did.

The days passed too quickly, and with every step closer to the duel, the castle buzzed louder with speculation and whispers of who would emerge the victor. Nefarious's name was on the lips of many, his size and experience often noted with grim admiration. But there were others, quieter voices, who believed in Calira—believed that his cunning and resolve would prove greater than brute strength alone. And I clung to those voices, hoping that they were right.

On the eve of the duel, as the moon hung heavy and full in the sky, I stood by the window of Calira's chambers, staring out at the shadowed world beyond the castle walls. The night was still, as if the world itself were holding its breath. Calira approached from behind, wrapping his arms around me, and for a moment, the fear melted away. In his embrace, I felt safe, as though nothing could tear us apart. But as the duel approached, I knew that safety was fleeting, and tomorrow would test more than just his strength. It would test the bond between us, and my heart could only hope it would not be broken.

"Tonisa," Calira's voice was soft as he approached, his hand resting lightly on my shoulder. There was a tenderness in his gaze that he rarely showed to anyone but me, a quiet vulnerability hidden beneath his calm strength. "I need to take to the sky."

I turned to face him, and though I tried to keep my expression neutral, I knew he could see the flicker of worry in my eyes. His hand slipped down to cup my face gently, his thumb brushing against my cheek. "Let's be honest," he continued, his voice steady but tinged with the weight of what was to come. "I won't leave this battle without wounds. Nefarious is no small opponent, and I will need every advantage I can muster. We should gather the herbs that will ensure my victory." His lips curved into a faint smile. "And besides, I've always wanted to take you for a flight to Laz'monat. There, we will find all we need—and perhaps even more than that."

The name of Laz'monat stirred something inside me. It was a place spoken of in hushed tones, a distant land known for its ancient wisdom and potent remedies. But more than that, it was the land of dragons, where the skies were said to be endless and the mountains held secrets long forgotten. To fly there with him, to witness the beauty of the world from the back of a dragon's wings, was something I had only dreamed of.

I couldn't help but smile, despite the tension that still clung to the air between us. "You're right," I said, nodding in agreement. "A dragon needs to stretch his wings before a fight." The words felt like a promise—a promise of strength, of defiance against the fear that gnawed at the edges of my heart.

Calira's smile grew, his eyes glinting with that familiar spark of adventure. "And what better way to prepare than to fly with you at my back?"

The thought sent a thrill through me, my blood singing with anticipation. To be with him, soaring through the sky, feeling the wind whip through my hair as we flew over mountains and valleys—it was the kind of wonder I had always longed for. Any chance to be beside him, especially in moments like this, was a gift of glory, of shared purpose. And though the shadow of the duel loomed ahead, this would be a moment of escape, a chance to claim something beautiful before the chaos of battle descended.

"I will be your wings, Tonisa," he whispered, his voice filled with an emotion that made my heart swell. "And you will be my strength. Together, we'll find what we need in Laz'monat—and when the time comes, I will fight knowing that you believe in me."

Those words thrummed in my ears like a beautiful ballad, the echoes of Calira's promise filling my heart with a warmth that pushed away the shadows of fear. I had been successful—he knew without a doubt that my faith in him was unwavering. As he instructed me to meet him in the gardens, I felt the flutter of anticipation in my chest, knowing this secret moment would belong to just the two of us.

When I arrived, the garden was bathed in the soft silver glow of the moon, its light filtering through the branches of the towering trees. And there, in the heart of it all, stood Calira— dark, stygian, and magnificent beyond words. He towered over everything around him, a creature of myth made flesh, seventy feet tall with wings that could blot out the moon itself. His wingspan was vast, arcing high into the night sky like a living fortress, each leathery membrane gleaming faintly in the pale light. His length, nearly three times his height, was perfectly proportioned, a massive testament to the raw power and grace that defined him.

His body was a masterpiece of strength, every muscle beneath his ebony scales rippling with quiet energy. His hair, a cascade of obsidian silk, flowed down the length of his neck like an ethereal waterfall, each strand seeming to absorb the moonlight as if it were alive with its own magic. It was tamed, smooth, and beautiful in a way that felt at odds with his fierce, formidable appearance. He was a dragon in every sense of the word—both terrible and breathtaking.

But what held me in that moment, what sent my heart racing, were his eyes. They glowed like molten gold, filled with the excitement of what was to come and the raw power of his dragon form. When he looked at me, it was as though he could see right through to my soul, a gaze that promised everything—flight, freedom, and the fierce love that bound us together.

I couldn't help myself. I ran to him, the giddiness of the moment overpowering the trepidation I'd felt earlier. He lowered himself to the ground, his massive frame settling with a thunderous grace as his wings curled inward, creating a path for me to ascend. I paused for a moment, gazing up at him, and realized just how enormous he truly was. Climbing onto his back felt like an impossible feat, and I briefly wondered how I could do it without making a fool of myself.

He must have sensed my hesitation because his eyes gleamed with amusement, the soft rumble of a dragon's chuckle reverberating through the air. His wing, broad and sturdy, dipped toward the ground, offering me my only real option for mounting him. I took a breath, placing my hand on the smooth, cool scales of his wing and began my ascent, feeling the powerful muscles beneath shift slightly as I made my way up.

Of course, just as I feared, I stumbled. My foot slipped on one of the slick scales, and I flailed for a moment, catching myself before I could fall back to the ground. Calira let out a deep, rumbling laugh, a sound that echoed through the garden like distant thunder. It was a sound only a dragon could make, rich and full of humor, and I huffed in mock frustration, my cheeks warming with embarrassment.

"Enjoying yourself?" I muttered, glancing up at his gleaming eyes.

His laughter softened, but the amusement still lingered in his gaze as he dipped his head slightly. "Quite," his voice reverberated through my mind, a deep, soothing presence that carried the slightest hint of teasing.

Despite the playful exchange, I managed to clamber onto his back with a semi-graceful ease, falling into place between the ridges of his spine. His body was warm beneath me, the heat of his dragon form seeping through his scales and wrapping me in a comforting embrace. The wind shifted around us as he straightened, his wings unfurling once more, and the world seemed to shift with him—everything below felt distant, small, as though nothing could touch us up here.

Settled in my place atop him, I reached out to stroke the smooth scales along his neck, marveling at the way they gleamed in the moonlight. "Ready?" his voice rumbled again, a quiet question that held the promise of something extraordinary.

"Always," I whispered, my voice swallowed by the roaring wind. The word was a vow, a promise wrapped in the wild cadence of my heartbeat as it raced to match the tempo of his wings. He tilted his head, a ghost of a smile flickering in the darkness. And then, with a mighty thrust, we left the ground behind.

The world vanished in a blur of shadow and moonlight as we shot into the sky, the force of our ascent pressing me back against the solid line of his spine. I clutched tighter, feeling the raw power coil and release beneath my fingers, muscles taut with a strength that seemed to defy nature itself. His wings cut through the night air, each beat reverberating in my bones, sending shivers skittering down my spine. It was both terrifying and exhilarating, the sensation of being utterly weightless and yet bound to something unstoppable.

The earth fell away in a dizzying sweep, the forest below shrinking to a mere tangle of dark shapes and silvery treetops. Villages dotted the landscape like tiny, flickering embers, their warm lights fading until even the memory of them was swallowed by the night. Higher and higher we climbed, until the entire world seemed like a distant dream, far below us. The air turned thinner and sharper, biting at my cheeks, but I hardly noticed. We broke through the low-lying clouds, the mist parting in swirls of silken vapor, and suddenly we were alone in a vast sea of moonlit sky. Stars glittered like a thousand secrets against the velvet canvas, and the moon hung above us, pale and perfect—a silent, watchful sentinel. My breath caught at the beauty of it all, the vastness of the heavens stretching out in every direction.

We leveled out, and I loosened my grip slightly, just enough to lift my head and gaze around us. He flew with the effortless grace of a creature born for the skies, wings sweeping in powerful arcs that whispered through the air like a lover's caress. The wind whipped through my hair, tugging at the loose strands, but the chill didn't bother me. All I could feel was him—the solid, unyielding heat of his body against mine, the steady rhythm of his heartbeat where my hands pressed against him. It anchored me, keeping me from spinning away into the endless night.

And then he banked, tipping us into a graceful spiral that sent my pulse skittering. We dove, skimming along the tops of clouds, and the world became a blur of motion and sensation. My laughter broke free before I could stop it, mingling with the wild rush of wind. It felt reckless, dangerous—like testing the edge of a blade. But I wasn't afraid. Not with him.

"Do you trust me?" he called over his shoulder, his voice low and laced with a challenge.

"Always," I answered, and I meant it. He could have taken us higher, past the point of breath and reason, and I would have followed without question.

He laughed, a dark, thrilling sound that sent my heart into a freefall. Then, with a sudden snap of his wings, he folded them in and we plunged, plummeting through the sky like a fallen star. The ground rushed up to meet us in a blur of shadows and silver, the wind screaming in my ears. For a heartbeat, the world narrowed to just us—our bodies entwined, locked in a dizzying dance with gravity.

But just as I braced myself, he flared his wings wide, and we pulled up, skimming over the treetops in a burst of momentum. My breath came in gasps, heart hammering as we leveled out once more, gliding low and fast through the night.

He looked back, eyes glittering in the darkness. "Fearless, aren't you?" he murmured, something like admiration flickering in his gaze.

"Only with you," I whispered back, feeling the truth of it settle deep in my bones.

It did not take us long to reach Lasmonat; the journey felt like a fleeting moment, carried on the swift wings of Calira. His powerful form cut through the air with unmatched speed and agility, each beat of his wings sending gusts of wind howling through the night.

The entrance to Lasmonat's hidden cave loomed ahead, a jagged maw in the face of the rock that seemed to swallow the very light around it. He descended with practiced precision, the rhythmic hum of his wings slowing until we hovered just above the narrow ledge. With a final, graceful sweep, Calira folded his wings and touched down with a delicate, almost reverent grace that belied his power.

My legs trembled as I slid down from his back, the ground rising to meet me in a disorienting rush. I stumbled, the solid earth beneath my boots foreign and unsteady after the wild freedom of the sky. Every muscle ached with the lingering thrill of the ride, and for a heartbeat, I just stood there, breathing deeply, trying to steady the racing pulse in my veins.

Then, as if time itself held its breath, the air shimmered around us. The massive, scaled form of Calira blurred and shifted, magic dancing in the night like silvered lightning. Wings folded and melted into smooth, muscled shoulders; talons retracted into lean, strong fingers; the proud head of the dragon bowed and softened, the fearsome snout narrowing into the chiseled jawline of a man. Scales receded, skin darkened like burnished bronze, and in a matter of seconds, Calira the dragon was gone—replaced by the figure of a man who seemed to carry the same fierce, regal beauty in every line of his form.

He stood before me, tall and imposing, his presence more commanding even in this shape. Midnight hair tumbled over his brow, framing eyes that burned with the same intense, fire that they did in his dragon form. The transformation left me breathless, no less stunning for having seen it before.

I opened my mouth to speak, to say something—anything— but as the adrenaline ebbed, I felt my balance falter. My legs, still unsteady from our flight, buckled beneath me. I pitched forward, and before I could catch myself, strong arms encircled me, pulling me into his chest.

"Careful," he murmured, his voice a deep, soothing rumble that reverberated through me. One hand cradled the back of my head, fingers tangling gently in my wind-tossed hair, while the other wrapped securely around my waist, holding me steady.

Heat radiated from his skin, chasing away the mountain's chill. I looked up, breath hitching as I met his gaze—those molten eyes alight with something unreadable, something that made my heart skip a beat. The scent of him—smoke and pine and something wild—filled my senses, intoxicating. For a moment, I forgot the world around us, forgot the looming darkness of the cave, the danger that awaited in the depths of Lasmonat. There was only him, the solid warmth of his body against mine, and the steady, reassuring thrum of his heartbeat beneath my palms.

"Didn't think you'd be so eager to fall into my arms," he teased softly, his lips curving into a faint smile. But the concern lingered in his eyes, a shadow that belied his light tone.

"I—" I swallowed, trying to find words, to remember how to breathe. "I'm not used to the ground after flying like that."

"Hmm." His gaze swept over my face, lingering on my flushed cheeks. "Perhaps I should keep you in the air more often, then. You seem to thrive up there."

There was a note of pride in his voice, and it made something flutter in my chest. I tried to pull back, but he didn't release me, his hold firm and unyielding.

"We should—" I began, forcing myself to focus. "The tunnels—"

"I know," he interrupted softly, his thumb brushing a feather-light caress along my cheekbone. His touch sent a spark skittering through me, and I shivered despite myself.

"But you've just dismounted a dragon," he murmured, leaning closer until his breath fanned against my skin, warm and tinged with the scent of smoke. "You deserve a moment to find your feet again." The words were so gentle, so utterly at odds with the raw power that radiated from him. My heart clenched, and before I could stop myself, I reached up, pressing a hand to his chest. He was real—so very real—and I felt the truth of it in the steady rise and fall of his breath.

"Thank you," I whispered, letting my hand linger for just a heartbeat longer. Then I straightened, forcing myself to take a step back, to put some distance between us. "I'm fine now."

His smile was faint, a mere quirk of his lips, but it made something warm and fragile bloom in my chest. He nodded, stepping aside to let me compose myself. But as I turned to face the mouth of the cave, his presence still burned in my awareness, a steady, comforting flame against the encroaching darkness.

"Let's go," I murmured, my voice steadier now. He fell into step beside me, a silent, protective shadow as we approached the entrance to the tunnels. The air grew colder, sharper, but I didn't falter.

We made our way deeper into the yawning mouth of the cave, the darkness swallowing us whole. The walls narrowed, the air growing cooler and carrying the scent of wet stone and the faintest trace of something else—something old and potent that made the fine hairs on my arms rise. Calira moved with surefooted grace despite the cramped space, his shoulders brushing against the rough stone as he ducked low, his figure shifting fluidly from dragon-like strength to human elegance.

Halfway in, he paused, bending to retrieve a small bundle that had been tucked into a crevice in the rock. From within, he produced a torch and a pile of folded clothing. With a flick of his wrist, he sparked the torch to life, the sudden burst of flame casting flickering shadows across the walls. His face was half-illuminated, the warm light catching the curve of his jaw, the strong line of his nose, and those molten eyes that seemed to burn brighter than the flame itself.

I couldn't help but smile as I watched him unravel the fabric, his hands deft and practiced. "Do you always leave clothing at your disposal here, my love?" I teased lightly, arching a brow.

He glanced at me, a slow smile spreading across his face as he straightened, pulling a simple black tunic over his broad shoulders. It settled against his form, the dark fabric clinging to his chest and arms, accentuating the power coiled beneath. "Yes, I do," he murmured, his voice low and intimate, reverberating softly off the stone walls. "I often come here alone when I need time to think."

The words were gentle, but they carried a weight to them, an echo of something deeper. I stepped closer, watching him as he ran a hand through his hair, the strands catching the light like threads of midnight silk. There was a rawness in his gaze, a flicker of memory that made my heart ache.

"When you were first banished," he continued quietly, his eyes never leaving mine as we walked, "I came here often when I missed you."

The confession hung between us, filling the space with a poignant silence. I swallowed, my chest tightening. My exile—it had been a wound that neither of us had spoken of much, a scar we had tried to forget but never truly healed. Hearing him say it now, knowing that he had wandered these empty tunnels alone, haunted by my absence—it was like feeling the sting of that loss all over again.

"This place," he murmured, his gaze shifting past me to the darkened depths of the cavern, "the beauty inside it made me think of you. The way the light catches on the crystals, the way the magic hums through the air… it reminded me of the power that runs through your veins, the way you could turn even the darkest places into something magnificent."

My breath caught. I glanced around, trying to see what he saw, but all I could make out were the jagged walls of stone, the uneven floor beneath our feet. But then he turned, raising the torch higher, and the flame's glow seemed to ripple and shift, casting strange, shimmering reflections across the rock.

Slowly, as if coaxed by his presence, the walls began to glisten, the shadows peeling back to reveal veins of crystalline minerals embedded deep within the stone. They shimmered softly, like the gleam of stars trapped in the rock, each flicker of light sending a cascade of iridescent colors dancing across the cave. The air itself seemed to hum in response, charged with a subtle, pulsing energy that thrummed through my bones, making my skin prickle.

"It's beautiful," I whispered, unable to tear my gaze away.

"Yes," he agreed softly, stepping closer until the warmth of his body pressed against my side. "Just like you."

The words were so simple, so sincere, that I couldn't help the way my heart tightened. He reached out, tracing a finger along the shimmering surface of the wall, his touch light and reverent. "The magic here… it's ancient. Unchanging. It's been here long before either of us were born, and it will be here long after we're gone. But in all that time, it never stops shining." He turned back to me, his expression solemn. "No matter what shadows fall, no matter what darkness tries to claim it, the light remains."

For a long moment, I couldn't breathe. There was something in his gaze—something raw and unguarded that made my chest constrict. I reached out, my fingers brushing his, and the warmth of his skin sent a shiver racing up my arm.

"I never knew you came here," I murmured softly, the words barely more than a breath. "That you—"

"Thought of you?" His smile was faint, almost wistful. "You were always with me, even when you were far away. Every time I saw the light, I thought of you. You were the fire in the darkness, the hope that refused to be snuffed out."

Emotion tightened my throat, and I blinked, forcing back the sudden sting of tears. I had been alone, lost in a world that seemed bent on breaking me. But he had been here, in this hidden sanctuary, finding solace in the echoes of my memory.

"I'm here now," I whispered, lifting my hand to cup his cheek, my thumb brushing gently along the strong line of his jaw. "I'm here, and I'm not going anywhere."

His gaze softened, something fragile and fierce flickering in the depths of his eyes. He turned his head, pressing a kiss to my palm, and I felt the faint tremor that ran through him, the way his breath hitched as if he couldn't quite believe it.

"Good," he murmured, his voice rough and unsteady. "Because I won't let you go. Not again."

SEVENTEEN

As we left the dark, winding trails of the cave and stepped into the vast expanse of Lasmonat, the world around us seemed to exhale, coming to life in a rush of magic and color. The air itself thrummed with energy, the lingering coolness of the cavern melting away as a breathtaking panorama unfolded before us—a hidden paradise, veiled beneath the bones of our world.

A hundred cascading waterfalls shimmered in the distance, their waters glowing with a soft, ethereal light that caught in the crystalline air, casting faint rainbows that shimmered like fragile threads of dreams. Rivulets streamed down jagged cliffs and wove between clusters of rocks that hovered weightlessly above the ground. Each stone, each shard, was a masterpiece of nature—floating gemstones and luminous crystals that pulsed gently with hues of indigo, emerald, and gold, casting the entire chamber in a kaleidoscope of colors.

My breath caught in my throat as I gazed out, taking in the sweeping view. The walls of the cavern soared impossibly high, arching up to a ceiling so distant that it vanished into shadows, the upper reaches lost in a web of drifting mist. And yet, from that darkness, a soft luminescence spilled down, bathing the entire landscape in a silvery glow, highlighting every delicate leaf, every ripple of water, every blade of grass that glowed with its own inner fire.

Trees spread out before us in sweeping groves, their branches trailing delicate tendrils of light, as if each leaf had been woven from strands of the stars themselves. They were massive, ancient things, their trunks thick and knotted with time, their roots spreading out like the veins of the earth. Their foliage shimmered in hues of violet and deep blue, the bioluminescence pulsating softly, as though each tree held a heartbeat, a life force that resonated with the magic in the air.

The path beneath our feet changed, the rough stone floor of the cave giving way to soft, fine sand that glittered faintly in the dim light. I looked down, half expecting to see ordinary sand, but instead found each grain glowing softly—a field of tiny, luminous particles, like crushed stardust scattered beneath our feet. As we walked, it shifted and swirled, forming delicate patterns that rippled outward, mimicking the movement of the stars in a midnight sky.

It was a place of dreams and wonders, a realm that seemed too beautiful, too fragile to be real. And yet, here it was, a hidden sanctuary locked beneath Evernia's crust, buried so deep that only a few knew of its existence. A world within a world, untouched and unseen, a place that whispered of secrets and stories that stretched back to the dawn of time.

Beside me, Calira remained silent, his eyes soft as he took in the scene. He had told me that this place reminded him of me—of the light I carried, the magic that ran through my veins. But standing here now, I couldn't help but feel that it was him this place mirrored. The strength, the power, the quiet, unwavering beauty that hid beneath the surface.

We walked further, our steps almost reverent, and the air grew warmer, tinged with the scent of something sweet and wild. Somewhere in the distance, a bird cried out—a high, lilting call that echoed through the cavern. My gaze followed the sound, and I spotted creatures darting between the glowing trees: small, delicate beings with wings like glass, their bodies flickering with iridescent light.

But it was what lay at the heart of Lasmonat that drew my gaze, capturing my breath in a moment of pure wonder. There, in the very center of the cavern, stood a grand platform—a raised dais of smooth, polished stone, its surface etched with intricate runes that glowed faintly. Energy crackled around it, shimmering in a soft, pulsating halo, and at its core hovered a gateway—an archway of swirling light and shadow, a portal that seemed to breathe and shimmer like a living thing.

The Platform of Transcendence. The name whispered through my mind, sending a thrill of recognition skittering through me. I had heard of it—read about it in the old tomes, stories passed down through the ages. It was a gateway to other worlds, a portal that linked this hidden sanctuary to realms far beyond our own. Planets scattered across the cosmos, untouched by our wars, our pain, our history. Worlds of mystery and magic, waiting to be explored.

I turned, my gaze catching Calira's profile in the soft glow of the cavern. He stood tall and still beside me, his expression unreadable, but I could see the way his hands clenched and unclenched, as if caught between longing and restraint. He had told me that he had never used the portal—that his duty kept him tethered to Evernia, bound by honor and responsibility. And yet, as I looked at him now, I could see the faint flicker of yearning in his eyes, the way his gaze lingered on the swirling light of the gateway.

My heart tightened painfully in my chest, and for a moment, I was tempted—so tempted—to reach out, to take his hand and pull him with me through that shimmering portal. To leave it all behind—the battles, the burdens, the weight of our titles. We could step through, together, and find ourselves on some distant star, in a world untouched by the chaos of our past. We could be free.

But I knew—gods, I knew—that it could never be that simple. He was a prince, bound by his people's expectations, his loyalty unbreakable. And if I was to be his queen someday, I could not ask him to run. I could not be the one who dragged him away from everything he had sworn to protect. The thought of it—of turning my back on this world, on our duty—was a sweet, bitter ache.

"We could leave," I whispered softly, the words barely more than a breath. "We could step through, you and I. Just... disappear. No one would ever find us."

He looked at me then, and the raw, open longing in his eyes made my heart ache. For a long moment, he didn't speak, his gaze locked on mine, the silence between us stretching taut and fragile.

"I would go," he murmured finally, his voice rough, aching. "If you asked me—if you truly asked me—I would go, and I would never look back."

I swallowed hard, my throat tight. "Calira—"

"But I know," he continued, a sad smile curving his lips, "that you would never ask."

And he was right. Because I knew—deep down, in the very core of my being—that to ask him to leave would be to shatter the very man I had fallen in love with. He was bound to this world, to its people, its future. And if I was to be by his side, then I, too, must learn to be strong enough to stay.

One day, perhaps, we would walk through that portal—side by side, with our duty fulfilled, our burdens set down. But until then... we would remain here. Together. In this world, this fragile, beautiful world, fighting for a future we could only dream of.

"I won't ask," I whispered, stepping closer, my fingers brushing against his. "Not yet."

His gaze softened, and he turned his hand, entwining his fingers with mine. "Then we stay."

And so we stood, hand in hand, staring out at the swirling portal—the gateway to a thousand possibilities, a thousand worlds we might never see. But for now, in this moment, it was enough.

Because we were here. Together. And that was where we belonged.

I didn't waste a moment gathering the supplies I would need for the trial that awaited us. Every second felt heavy, each heartbeat a reminder of what was at stake. My hands moved swiftly, plucking the delicate, shimmering blossoms of the Essence of Vlover from the tangled undergrowth. The petals, a soft violet hue, trembled under my touch, releasing a faint, sweet fragrance that made my senses sharpen. Vlover was a rare find, its essence potent enough to amplify the healing properties of most other herbs, but only if prepared correctly. I placed each blossom carefully into a small, sealed vial, ensuring not a single drop of its vital nectar would be lost.

Next was the Stem of Bailblight. The plant itself was thorny, its tendrils twisting and writhing like something out of a nightmare. A single touch from its barbed spines would send most fleeing with searing pain, but I had no such luxury. I pulled on my gloves—thick leather lined with enchanted runes—and wielded my knife with steady precision. The dark, woody stem snapped free with a muted crack, its bark oozing a thick, inky sap. Bailblight was known for its properties of resilience, its essence capable of hardening the skin like armor for a few precious minutes—crucial moments that could mean the difference between life and death.

I glanced up, my gaze flitting around the clearing as if expecting to see danger lurking in the shadows. But the forest remained still, the only sound the whisper of leaves in the soft breeze. My chest tightened, a knot of anxiety coiling beneath my ribs. I forced myself to breathe deeply and focused on my task.

The Leaves of Everil were next. The plant was fragile, its slender leaves nearly translucent in the dim light of the grove. A soft, silvery glow radiated from its edges, and I knew that even the slightest mishandling could render its magical properties useless. Everil was prized for its restorative abilities, capable of mending broken bones and knitting torn flesh in the blink of an eye. But its potency was volatile, the magic within it delicate and fickle. I gathered a handful of the leaves with utmost care, folding them gently and wrapping them in soft cloth before tucking them into the satchel.

Finally, I turned my attention to the Roots of the Bloodstanch Tree. The most dangerous of them all. Bloodstanch trees only grew in the deepest parts of the woods, their dark crimson bark twisting like sinew around the base of massive trunks. The roots, thick and gnarled, had to be harvested with exacting precision. One wrong cut and the essence within would spoil, turning from a lifesaving elixir into a lethal poison. I knelt beside the tree's base, feeling the pulse of magic thrumming through the earth as I dug my fingers into the soil.

The roots twisted under my touch, resisting, as if aware of my intent. I murmured softly, coaxing the plant with a quiet, soothing chant. The magic responded slowly, reluctantly, and I slid my blade along the base of the root, severing it with a single, clean slice. The root shuddered, and then stilled, a dark, ruby-red liquid oozing from the cut. I quickly collected it into a small crystal vial, corking it tightly.

The Bloodstanch was powerful—able to halt even the worst bleeding in an instant. But it was also unpredictable. Too much would render the user immobile, their body paralyzed by the overwhelming force of its magic. Too little, and it would be no more useful than water. I had seen skilled healers use it and fail, the balance between life and death a razor's edge. I hoped I would not have to use it on Calira. I prayed that I would not have to use it at all.

With the final vial secured, I stood, surveying my work. My satchel bulged with the weight of the supplies, the vials clinking softly as I adjusted the strap over my shoulder. Each ingredient was essential, a vital piece of the arsenal I would need should the unthinkable happen. Calira was a dragon—immense, powerful, seemingly indestructible. But I had seen even the greatest of creatures fall in battle, their strength broken by the cruelty of fate. And while every part of me screamed that he would rise victorious, unscathed… I could not afford to be unprepared.

"Everything ready?" His voice, low and smooth, pulled me from my thoughts. I turned to find him watching me from the edge of the grove, his silhouette outlined in the faint, dappled light. In his human form, he looked almost deceptively ordinary, his broad shoulders and calm demeanor giving no indication of the beast that lurked beneath his skin. But his eyes—the molten red of his gaze burned with intensity, a fire that no mortal shell could contain.

"Yes," I said quietly, adjusting the strap of the satchel once more. "I have everything we might need."

His gaze shifted to the bulging satchel, a wry smile tugging at the corner of his lips. "You've brought enough to heal an entire army."

"Or to protect one dragon," I shot back softly, the words sharper than I intended.

His smile faded, replaced by something far more serious. He crossed the distance between us in two long strides, his hands cupping my face, tilting my head up until I was forced to meet his gaze. "You won't need any of this," he murmured, his thumbs brushing gently along my cheeks. "I'll come back to you. Whole. I promise."

I wanted to believe him. Gods, I wanted to believe with every fiber of my being. But promises were fragile things, easily broken by the harsh reality of battle. Still, I forced myself to nod, to lean into his touch, letting his warmth chase away the chill that had settled in my bones.

"And if you don't?" I whispered, the question slipping out before I could stop it.

His eyes softened, "Then you'll save me, as you always do."

I swallowed, fighting the urge to close my eyes, to lose myself in the comfort of his touch. "And if I can't?"

"Then you'll still be the last thing I see," he murmured, pressing his forehead against mine, his breath warm against my skin. "And that, my love, is more than I could ever ask for."

Tears stung my eyes, but I blinked them away, forcing myself to smile, to be strong—for him, if not for myself. "You'll come back," I whispered fiercely, willing it to be true. "You will."

His lips brushed mine, a fleeting, featherlight kiss. "I will," he vowed softly. "For you, I will always come back."

And then, before I could reply, he swept me into his arms, lifting me effortlessly as if I weighed nothing at all. A surprised laugh escaped my lips, but it was quickly swallowed by the intensity of his gaze. He carried me toward the nearest tree, its ancient trunk twisted and strong, offering shelter beneath its sprawling branches.

He set me down gently, my back pressing against the rough bark, the contrast sending a thrill coursing through me. With deliberate slowness, he traced his fingers along the curve of my cheek, his touch igniting sparks that danced across my skin. His eyes searched mine, seeking permission, a silent question hanging in the air between us.

Before I could catch my breath, he knelt before me, his hands gathering the fabric of my skirts. The world seemed to hold its breath as he lifted the layers, the cool air brushing against my legs. A flush warmed my cheeks, anticipation and desire swirling in a heady mix. His lips brushed against the sensitive skin of my inner thigh, a feather-light touch that made me shiver.

I carefully set the satchel aside, letting it slip from my shoulder to rest safely away from us. The weight of it was nothing compared to the gravity of this moment. My fingers found their way into his hair, the strands slipping like silk between them. I surrendered to the tide of emotions rising within me, my defenses melting away under the warmth of his touch.

He looked up at me, his eyes filled with a tenderness that stole my breath. "Trust me," he whispered, his voice barely more than a murmur.

"Always," I replied, my voice steady despite the fluttering in my chest.

He smiled then—a soft, genuine smile that reached his eyes—and resumed his tender exploration. Each kiss, each caress was a silent vow, a promise etched into the very fabric of our beings. The forest around us faded into a blur of color and light; there was only the two of us, wrapped in this stolen moment.

Leaves rustled overhead, and somewhere in the distance, a bird sang a solitary note. Time seemed to slow, each heartbeat echoing loudly in my ears. I felt connected—to him, to the earth beneath us, to the very essence of life that pulsed in every living thing around us.

As the boundaries between us blurred, my legs parted for him and I felt the fork of his tongue tracing the lines of my lips. My temple eager and wet for him summoned him like a bee to honey and in the night I allowed him to feast.

EIGHTEEN

The day of the duel dawned with a sense of foreboding that gripped the entire kingdom. The sky was painted in stormy shades of charcoal and indigo, casting eerie shadows over the battlements and the gathered throngs below. The great castle, nestled atop the highest cliff of the region, stood sentinel over the arena where two forces of nature were set to collide. Even the castle's tallest spires seemed dwarfed by the titanic presence of the two dragons standing poised for battle in the courtyard below.

To the left, Calira, a monstrous beast of shadow and fire, towered over the crowd, his scales blacker than the deepest abyss. Each obsidian plate shimmered faintly under the dull light, like liquid darkness hardened into armor. His wings, crimson as freshly spilled blood, were arched high above him, their translucent membranes glowing like stained glass in the muted morning. The spines along his back, razor-sharp and jagged, flared with a menacing glint, and his massive talons gouged deep furrows into the ancient stones beneath him as he shifted, the ground trembling with the weight of his power. Smoke curled from his nostrils, carrying the acrid scent of sulfur and ash, and his eyes burned with a predatory hunger. Calira was the embodiment of fury and vengeance, a warlord among dragons.

Opposite him stood his rival, Prince Nefarious Argon'atsu, a creature of startling, terrible beauty. His scales shimmered in a brilliant shade of emerald green, each one reflecting the light like a precious jewel, and the gold-flecked wings that spread wide behind him seemed to capture and hold the very essence of sunlight. But it was his eyes—those twin orbs of pure, molten gold—that drew every gaze and held it fast. They blazed with an unholy intensity, their light dancing with cunning and malevolence. Embedded along his spine and shoulders were countless emeralds, each gemstone set with meticulous precision into his scales, glowing faintly like enchanted beacons. They pulsed with hidden magic, threads of energy that wove through his powerful body and gathered around his outstretched claws. Here was no ordinary dragon but a creature bound to dark sorceries, a prince of war and ruin.

And I, Tonisa, stood watching from a balcony high above, my heart hammering in my chest as the two colossal beings squared off. I clutched the stone railing, feeling its cold bite against my palms as I leaned forward. Even from this distance, I could sense the raw, unbridled power radiating from both dragons—a power that shook the very foundations of the castle and sent shivers of fear racing through the assembled crowd.

The onlookers, a mix of noble lords, guards, and commoners, stood silent and awestruck. The bravest among them dared to look upon the dueling pair, while others turned away, hiding their faces behind trembling hands. For no one could forget the devastation such creatures could unleash. Stories of entire villages laid to waste and armies incinerated by a single exhale of draconic breath filled every whispered tale. Yet today, they were not just witnesses to such might; they were caught between two living tempests about to clash in a storm of fire and fury.

"By the gods," I murmured, more to myself than to anyone nearby. "What madness drives them to this?" My voice was almost lost in the wind, but still, I could feel the weight of my own words settle heavy on my heart.

Calira's head swung in my direction, his keen eyes locking with mine for the briefest of moments. A strange stillness settled over me. The black dragon—my closest ally, my fiercest protector—held my gaze, a flicker of something unspoken passing between us. Did he seek reassurance? Or perhaps a silent promise that I would not look away, no matter what was to come?

But the moment shattered as Prince Argon'atsu's voice rumbled across the courtyard, low and mocking, reverberating through the stones like an ominous drumbeat.

"Calira of the Ebon Flame," he growled, his tone a silken blend of disdain and dark amusement. "You dare face me, stripped of your kin, shorn of your crown? I expected more grandeur for your last stand."

Calira's lips peeled back in a snarl, exposing rows of gleaming fangs like jagged blades. His growl reverberated through the courtyard, a deep, primal sound that made the very air vibrate. "And I expected less pomp for a self-proclaimed prince weighed down by trinkets and baubles," he retorted, his voice a dangerous rumble that promised pain and retribution.

The green dragon's wings flared wide, catching the faintest hint of sunlight and scattering emerald light across the stones. He bared his own fangs in a twisted grin, his eyes glinting with cruel delight. "Then let us see whose fire burns brighter. Let us see whose strength is greater."

A hush fell over the courtyard. The wind died, and time seemed to hang suspended in a fragile, breathless moment. Then, with a sudden, violent explosion of movement, they launched at each other.

Calira's wings snapped out, propelling him forward like a bolt of shadowed lightning. Nefarious met him head-on, his emerald scales shimmering like a verdant blaze against Calira's dark silhouette. They collided with a thunderous crash that shook the castle walls, claws and fangs tearing, wings beating furiously as they grappled and twisted in a deadly dance of fury and flame.

The courtyard erupted in chaos as the dragons battled, their roars shaking the very sky. Calira's black wings flared crimson, sweeping out to buffet Nefarious back, while the green dragon's own wings struck like a viper's coils, their edges sharp as knives. Sparks flew as their scales clashed, emerald and obsidian blurring together in a whirlwind of raw power. The scent of brimstone and scorched stone filled the air as Calira's jaws snapped forward, blazing fire spilling from his maw in a torrent of red-hot flame.

But Nefarious was quick—too quick. He twisted sharply, his own fire—a searing jet of emerald flame—answering Calira's attack. Their flames met in midair, an inferno of red and green that seared the sky and cast wild, flickering shadows over the stunned crowd below.

And I, high above, could only watch as the titans clashed, their fury shaking the world around them. My heart pounded in my chest, torn between terror and awe. For this was no mere duel. This was a war of wills, a clash of destinies, and somewhere in the fire and the chaos, the fate of more than just these two mighty creatures would be decided.

The pair took to the sky, locking their talons together as they spun upward, twisting and snarling in an aerial dance of death. Calira's roar shook the heavens, deep and rumbling like the coming of a storm, while Nefarious's shriek cut through the air like shattered glass. The earth itself seemed to tremble beneath them as they fought for dominance, their massive bodies rolling through the sky, darkening the horizon.

Calira lashed out with his spiked tail, striking Nefarious across the face. Blood, thick and black as tar, sprayed into the air, glistening in the firelight. Nefarious hissed, his green eyes narrowing with murderous intent as he wrenched free, twisting his body with such force that Calira was flung backward. The black dragon's wings beat furiously, stabilizing himself just as Nefarious lunged again, his razor-sharp teeth snapping at Calira's neck.

There was a sound—a sickening crack—as Nefarious's jaws closed around one of Calira's horns, snapping it clean off. A roar of agony burst from Calira's throat, and he retaliated with a brutal swipe of his claws, ripping through Nefarious's underbelly. The green dragon shrieked, reeling backward as his emerald blood rained down like molten metal, sizzling where it struck the stone courtyard below.

But neither dragon showed any sign of retreat. They were too deep into the madness of battle, too consumed by rage. With another thunderous bellow, they charged at each other once more, a clash of talons and teeth and fire. Calira's remaining horn gleamed in the firelight, and with a mighty thrust, he impaled it deep into Nefarious's side.

Nefarious screamed, his wings flapping wildly as he struggled to break free. The two dragons plummeted toward the earth, locked together in a deadly embrace, their combined weight sending shockwaves through the ground as they crashed into the courtyard below. The impact was like the breaking of mountains, the stone shattering beneath them as they rolled in a tangled heap of blood and fury. For a moment, there was only silence—the eerie stillness of two great beasts gasping for breath, their bodies broken and bloodied.

Then, with one last, desperate effort, Calira heaved himself upward, his jaws closing around Nefarious's throat. The green dragon's eyes widened in terror, his wings twitching feebly as he struggled against the inevitable.

Calira's teeth sank deeper, and the taste of blood flooded his senses, igniting a primal satisfaction. The heat of battle surged through him, the power of the kill within reach. Nefarious let out a strangled gasp, his green eyes wide with panic, talons scrabbling for purchase on the ruined courtyard below. But just as the final deathblow seemed inevitable, the green dragon lifted his wing straight up into the air, trembling as it waved—a sign unmistakable even in the throes of combat. He was asking for mercy.

For a heartbeat, everything stood still. The crowd below, who had been watching in horrified awe, gasped in unison. The two mighty dragons hung suspended in a fragile moment where the future of their kind seemed to teeter on the edge of that lifted wing. Nefarious, proud and relentless only moments before, now lay broken, submitting himself to the judgment of his adversary.

Calira's jaws remained clamped, his sharp teeth still piercing Nefarious's neck. The temptation to finish it—to sever the life from his rival and claim his place as the sole ruler of the skies—burned hot in his chest. But something deeper stirred in the black dragon, a flicker of ancient memory, of battles fought in the old ways, where to grant mercy was a show of true strength, where victory wasn't measured by slaughter alone.

Slowly, with a low growl that rumbled like distant thunder, Calira loosened his grip, letting Nefarious's throat slide free from his bloodstained jaws. The green dragon slumped to the ground, gasping for breath, his wings trembling with pain and exhaustion.

But there would be no rest. With one swift, brutal movement, Calira stepped forward, planting his massive taloned foot on Nefarious's face, pinning the defeated dragon to the cracked stone below. The impact sent a ripple of cracks through the already broken courtyard, dust rising in lazy swirls around the dragons' colossal forms. Nefarious groaned, his great body shuddering beneath the weight of his conqueror.

Then, Calira lifted his head high, his crimson-black wings flaring wide as he threw back his neck and unleashed a roar that shattered the skies. It was a roar not of mere victory, but of dominance, of a power that echoed from the deepest roots of the world itself. The sound surged through the air, vibrating the very bones of those who watched, as though the earth itself bent to his will. The wind whipped around him, tearing at the banners on the towers, and the sky itself seemed to darken in response, as if nature understood that one of its greatest titans had claimed his throne.

From above, I could feel the weight of Calira's triumph, his roar a proclamation that resonated not just in the physical realm but deep within the hearts of all who bore witness. There was no denying it: Calira had won. The skies, the land, even the future trembled beneath his might.

Nefarious, once proud, now lay battered and bloodied beneath the black dragon's foot, his emerald scales dulled by blood and dirt, his chest heaving weakly. He had been spared—but he would live the rest of his life as a reminder of this defeat, of his submission. The weight of humiliation was perhaps heavier than any wound Calira could have inflicted.

And yet, in that mercy, there was something more terrifying than death itself. Calira had shown restraint, not out of kindness, but because he knew that true power was not in destroying one's enemy completely—it was in letting them live to witness their own ruin. Nefarious's survival was not salvation. It was a curse.

The crowd below remained silent, too awestruck to cheer or even breathe. They knew they had witnessed something more than a battle—they had witnessed the reshaping of the world's balance. The age of Nefarious had ended. And from the ashes of his defeat, a new era had risen, one ruled by the black dragon whose wings now stretched wide across the sky.

Calira's roar faded into the wind, but its echoes would live on for centuries, carried on the breath of legends. He looked down at Nefarious one last time, a flicker of contempt in his burning eyes, before lifting his foot from the vanquished dragon's face. Without a word, Calira turned and leapt into the sky, his powerful wings beating the air as he soared into the heavens, his shadow cast long and dark over the broken world below.

The crowd remained frozen, the silence heavy as they watched the black dragon disappear into the clouds. And as Nefarious lay in the rubble, broken and bleeding, it became clear to all: this was no mere victory. This was the dawn of a new reign, and the world would never be the same again.

NINETEEN

For two agonizing days, I waited, the hours dragging on like an eternity as I stood on the precipice of hope and despair. Calira had vanished without a word, leaving me with nothing but the silence of unanswered questions and the hollow ache of his absence. I didn't know where he had gone, nor the reason for his sudden departure, but I clung to the fragile hope that when he returned, he would carry with him the answers that eluded me.

When at last he appeared, my heart soared, relief flooding through me like the first breath of spring after a bitter winter. Yet, even in my joy, a darker part of me whispered thanks to the gods for the wounds he bore. They were grievous enough to demand my care but not so dire as to steal him away from me entirely. His life, though hanging in a precarious balance, was still within my grasp to save. The infection lurking in his flesh posed a grave threat, but it was a danger I could ward off, a battle I was prepared to fight with every ounce of strength I had left.

He returned not as the fearsome dragon I had come to know, but as a man—his human form weary, broken, and bleeding. The most grievous of his wounds was a savage gash on the left side of his temple, where Nefarious had ripped his horn clean off in their brutal battle. Blood matted his dark hair, and the angry wound throbbed beneath the fading light. His neck and torso bore deep, angry gashes, jagged reminders of the fight.

But there were other marks upon him, ones I did not recognize from the battle with Nefarious. They were strange, foreign—scratches and bruises that stirred a cold dread within me. Yet before I could reach him, another did. Alexandria.

She rushed to him, her loyalty like a dagger to my heart as she embraced him, her lips trailing soft, reverent kisses along his battered skin. I watched, my stomach twisting into knots as her delicate hands framed his face, her tears spilling freely for him. She wept as if her heart was breaking, but it wasn't her grief that crushed me—it was the fact that he held her so tenderly.

Even as his arms encircled her, there was no tenderness in the way he held her. No gentle press of fingers, no soothing words whispered to calm her sobs. His touch, once so full of passion and fire, now seemed perfunctory, as if his hands were simply going through the motions. His gaze, fixed over her shoulder, was distant, void of the warmth that once lingered there. It was a gaze I had never seen directed at me—until now.

As our eyes met across the space between us, the truth settled over me like the hush of a winter's night. His expression was unreadable, cold and unmoving as stone, but I saw it—the flicker beneath that impassive mask, the quiet storm raging behind his eyes. He was no longer the man who once loved her. That love, once fierce and unbreakable, had long withered into nothing but dust, scattered by the winds of time and the battles he had fought, both within and without.

And in that bitter silence, with the sounds of Alexandria's broken sobs muffled between us, the realization hit me like a tidal wave.

It was not her he yearned for anymore. It had never been her that brought him back from the brink. The depth of his love, the pull that had guided him home through pain and bloodshed, had always been for me.

The world shifted around me, my heart thudding painfully in my chest as the truth unfolded before me. It wasn't just the absence of love for her that I saw in his gaze—it was the quiet, undeniable presence of something far deeper. For me. His love, raw and unspoken, lay beneath the surface of that stoic expression, a bond forged in fire and darkness, stronger than the hollow ties that still bound him to his wife.

He didn't need to say it. He didn't need to move. In the silence, in the lock of our eyes, I felt it. He had returned to me, not as a warrior, not as the man bound to another, but as someone whose heart had always been mine. Even if neither of us had spoken it aloud, the truth was undeniable, shimmering in the air between us like a vow unspoken, a promise of what was yet to come.

I forced myself forward, each step a battle against the storm of emotions raging inside me. Every instinct screamed at me to tear her away from him, to claim what was mine, but I swallowed the bitter taste of jealousy and buried it deep. My hand trembled as I reached out, and instead of curling my fingers into claws, I placed them gently on the queen's shoulder.

It took everything within me not to dig my nails into her skin, to rip her from his embrace, but I kept my touch soft, deliberate, almost soothing. A gesture that spoke of understanding, of welcome, even as my heart twisted with every beat. I could feel the heat of his body through her, the tension thrumming just beneath the surface, and it made my breath catch. He hadn't pushed her away, not yet, but I could sense the growing distance between them, like a chasm widening with every passing second.

Her sobs stilled, her body trembling beneath my hand, and for a moment, she didn't move. She was still lost in her grief, in the false hope that his silence meant something more than it did. I knew better now. His love for her was as cold as the stone beneath our feet, as lifeless as the air between them. And while she clung to him with desperation, I felt it—his subtle shift, the weight of his attention moving from her to me. The invisible thread that had always tied us together tugged at him now, drawing him away from her and toward me.

I couldn't tear her away with force, but I didn't need to. He was already slipping from her grasp, even if she didn't realize it yet. My hand, still resting lightly on her shoulder, was an invitation, a promise of comfort. But it wasn't for her—it was for him. I had never needed to fight for him; he had always been mine, even if it had taken me until now to see it.

The queen's breath hitched, and as she slowly pulled back from him, I felt her crumbling. I had won, though I hadn't needed to raise a single weapon. He had made his choice long before this moment, and now, all that was left was for her to realize it too.

"Queen Alexandria, please, allow me to tend the king. His wounds have festered and must be tended." I spoke softly

She turned to face me, her swollen eyes red and raw from the weight of her tears. Her face, usually so poised, was now marred by grief and fury, her round cheeks flushed with a mixture of anguish and rage. For a moment, I thought she might speak, might lash out at me with words as sharp as any blade, but instead, she merely nodded, silent and broken.

Then her hands moved instinctively to her stomach, and a soft cry of pain escaped her lips. It was a pitiful sound, full of vulnerability, but I felt no pity. In that instant, something colder and darker settled over me, a reminder of the mission I had nearly forgotten in my rush to be at Calira's side.

The children.

Her hand rested protectively over the life growing within her, a symbol of everything that stood between me and the power, the glory, that was rightfully mine. My mind raced with the thought, my own heart hardening as I stared at her. If my child had been cast aside, discarded like an afterthought, then what right did hers have to live?

They were a threat, the final obstacle standing in my path. Calira had returned, his love no longer hers, but these unborn heirs still held sway, binding him to her, tethering him to a future that did not include me. I couldn't allow it. I wouldn't. These children, born of a marriage long devoid of true love, would never see the light of day. They could not.

My gaze flicked down to her rounded belly, and for the briefest moment, I almost felt the echo of the bond I had once carried within me. But it was fleeting, as cold and brittle as the winter wind. There was no room for mercy, not anymore. Her children would never replace mine. They were a danger to everything I had fought for, to the future I would claim. And I knew what had to be done.

The ache in her face, the pain she clutched at with every sob, only made it clearer—fate was already beginning to turn. Soon, the power she held through them would be severed, and Calira would be mine, free of the chains this woman and her heirs sought to place upon him. The time was coming, and with it, my glory.

"Yes, see to the king, for he is in need of your skill. As for me, I shall retire to my chambers. The weight of this day has been far too great, and I fear it has taken its toll upon both myself and the babes I carry. When you have tended to His Majesty's wounds, come to me at once. I would have your presence and care, for I find myself in need of both comfort and company this eve."

"Of course, Queen Alexandria, I will be sure both you and the king's heir are properly tended."

Satisfied with my compliance, the queen turned sharply on her heel, her gown whispering across the stone floor as she made her way toward her chambers. The weight of her command lingered in the air, but I scarcely noticed her retreat, for my attention was wholly drawn to Calira. His strength had faltered, and I quickly stepped beneath his arm, steadying his broad frame as he leaned heavily into me. The scent of blood and earth clung to him, a reminder of the battle that had nearly stolen him away. His body was battered, but it was his spirit I feared for most.

The servants, lingering like specters in the hall, watched in silence, their eyes wide and uncertain. They made no move to help, for their loyalty lay with the queen, and her absence left a hollow void between us. Yet even as their gazes bore into me, it was not their presence that unnerved me.

To my left, a flicker of movement caught my attention. From the shadows, Rose watched, her figure half-concealed in the dim light of the corridor. A grim smile spread slowly across her lips, her eyes gleaming with a knowledge she had yet to share. There was something unsettling in the way she observed, like a predator waiting for the right moment to strike.

I opened my mouth to call out to her, my words forming on my tongue, but before I could utter a sound, she was gone, vanishing as swiftly as she had appeared, swallowed by the darkness. A chill skated down my spine, though I wasn't sure whether it was her disappearance or the eerie satisfaction in her gaze that unsettled me more.

With a steadying breath, I turned my focus back to Calira, tightening my grip around his waist as I guided him forward. The shadows in this place were growing deeper, and though the queen had retired, her presence—along with the dangerous games being played around us—was far from forgotten.

Something dark stirred beneath the surface, and with every step I took, I could feel the weight of it pressing down, tightening its hold on all of us. The queen's retreat, Rose's cryptic smile, the servants' silent watch—they were all pieces of a larger puzzle, one that was shifting, twisting, as fate began to draw its lines. And in the heart of it all was Calira—and me.

At long last, we crossed the threshold into his chambers, the door creaking shut behind us as if it, too, carried the weight of the moment. Without hesitation, I turned the key, the soft click of the lock sealing us in. The outside world faded into nothingness, and for the briefest heartbeat, desire roared to life within me, fierce and unbidden. I ached to claim him, to climb atop his battered form and lose myself in the heat of him. But I forced the temptation down, reminding myself there were more urgent matters that demanded my attention.

Calira sank heavily into the nearest chair, his body weary from battle and blood loss. His gaze, half-lidded with exhaustion, followed my movements, though he said nothing. The quiet between us hummed with unspoken tension, but I steeled myself, moving swiftly across the room.

The fire in the hearth crackled low, casting flickering shadows across the stone walls. I crouched before it, feeding fresh wood to the embers, stoking the flames until they raged anew. The warmth licked at my skin, but it was not enough to drive away the cold gnawing at the edges of my mind. There was so much at stake, so much that could unravel if I didn't act swiftly.

I gathered my materials with practiced hands—the herbs and poultices I had prepared, their pungent scents filling the air. The needles and horsehair thread lay neatly beside them, ready to stitch his torn flesh back together. My movements were methodical, efficient, but beneath my calm exterior, a storm brewed. Every touch, every breath, felt charged with meaning, as though the very air between us had thickened with the weight of what was to come.

I turned back to him, my eyes tracing the lines of his body—strong but broken, powerful yet vulnerable. The blood from his wounds had begun to dry, but I could see the deep gash near his temple where Nefarious had torn his horn away, and the other, smaller wounds that crisscrossed his torso like a map of his suffering.

For a moment, our gazes locked, and I saw in his eyes a flicker of something—something that mirrored the fire burning within me. But I could not give in to it, not yet. There would be time for that later, when the battle for his life had been won.

Without a word, I knelt before him, my hands trembling slightly as I reached for the herbs, preparing to cleanse his wounds. The scent of rosemary and yarrow filled the room, mingling with the smoke from the hearth, creating an almost sacred atmosphere. This was not just the tending of wounds; it was an act of devotion, a vow of protection that I made silently to him.

"Tonisa…" He spoke gently.

"Hush now, don't speak. I must flush and tend these wounds lest you succumb to infection after such a great victory."

His hand slid into my hair, his fingers threading through the strands before giving a gentle, possessive squeeze. The sudden contact sent a shiver down my spine, tethering me to the moment. His voice, low and rough, broke the silence between us.

"We must speak now," he murmured, his tone laden with urgency. "Here, where no ears can pry and no one can learn of our plans."

I met his gaze, searching for the weight behind his words, and in his eyes, I found it—a storm of emotions barely held in check, the same storm that had raged within me since his return. He was a man divided, torn between the battlefield of his heart and the one that lay ahead of us.

"If you've wondered where I've been," he continued, his voice tightening with the strain of whatever secret he carried, "I flew to Lazmonat after the fight. I needed to clear my mind, to seek the guidance I could not find here. To know what I must do next."

His thumb brushed lightly against my scalp, his touch both grounding and electrifying. My thoughts spun, questions rising like a tide within me—why Lazmonat? What guidance had he sought there? And most of all, what did it mean for us?

But I held my tongue, sensing that he was not finished, that there was more he needed to reveal before I could even begin to ask. The fire in the hearth crackled, the warmth of it contrasting sharply with the coolness of his revelations. We were alone now, locked in a chamber where the world outside could not touch us, but the weight of what he had done—and what he would do—pressed heavily against the walls.

I shifted closer, my pulse thrumming in my ears, bracing for whatever truth was about to unfold. We were standing on the edge of something vast, something that would change the course of everything. And I could feel that, whatever came next, our fates were bound irrevocably together.

I gently pulled away from his touch, the weight of his words lingering between us, but I could not afford to lose focus. The sharp edge of purpose cut through the haze of desire that threatened to cloud my mind. I moved to the small basin, pouring water into a pot and adding a generous measure of salt. The fire hissed and crackled as the water heated, steam curling into the air, but my thoughts were already turning back to him.

When the water had boiled and cooled enough to be safe, I returned to his side. His eyes were dark, locked on me, watching my every move as though weighing my resolve. With a steady hand, I soaked a cloth and began flushing the deep gashes across his torso. He growled in protest, his muscles tensing beneath my touch, but I didn't falter.

"Be still," I murmured, my tone firm yet soft, as though taming a restless beast. "These wounds will fester if left uncleansed."

He glared at me, but the fight in his eyes dimmed as I continued. The wounds were filthy—grit and sand embedded in the torn flesh, mixed with leaves and the remnants of battle. The water, stained red, dripped away, revealing healthy, unmarred skin beneath the grime. Only when the last of the dirt was washed away, and his body lay clean before me, did I begin the careful work of stitching him back together.

I threaded the needle with horsehair, the tip gleaming in the firelight as I drew it through his skin. His jaw tightened, a grimace pulling at his features, but still, he continued to speak through the pain.

"Tonisa," he rasped, his voice low and rough. "I sought the guidance of the gods... and they have shown me the path I must take."

I paused, the thread held taut between my fingers, my heart thudding in my chest. His words hung in the air, heavy with meaning, with destiny. He drew a breath, and when he spoke again, his voice was resolute.

"They showed me that you are to be my wife. My queen." His eyes locked with mine, unwavering, and for a moment, I felt the gravity of that truth pull me in. "But Alexandria... she stands in our way."

The name struck like a blade, sharp and cold, reminding me of the reality that lay between us. The queen, with her loyalty, her lineage, her claim to him—and the children she carried. My hands trembled for a brief second, but I steadied myself. My stitching never faltered, though my mind raced.

I knew this day would come, knew the bond between Calira and Alexandria was as fragile as a cobweb, ready to snap. But hearing it spoken aloud, with the authority of the gods behind it, was something altogether different.

I tied off the final stitch, smoothing the line of thread over his skin. The room seemed to hold its breath as I rose, moving closer to him. His wounds were bound, but the wounds between us, the tangled web of love, power, and fate, had only just begun to reveal themselves.

"And what would you have me do?" I asked softly, though the question held far more weight than the words suggested.

"Despite the ruin it might bring upon my father and our house, I would ask of you the unthinkable. Alexandria must be removed—by whatever means you see fit. My own hand is bound, for I cannot move against her without risking everything. But yours... yours remains free to act where mine cannot."

He leaned forward, his voice dropping to a low murmur, the weight of his command heavy with both guilt and determination. "Make it so, and rid us of the obstacle that stands between us and the crown."

TWENTY

What Calira had asked of me was everything I had ever dreamed, a whispered promise of power and a future by his side. But dreams and reality seldom danced in harmony. I could not afford to act recklessly, not with so much at stake. To remove Alexandria, the queen who held the fragile peace between the dragon clans in her grip, required more than brute force. If she were to simply turn up dead, suspicion would turn to us, and war would erupt, setting the entire realm aflame. No, her end had to be more subtle, more carefully orchestrated—a gradual descent into weakness, until she was nothing more than a shadow of the queen she once was.

I could not strike the final blow outright. Not yet. Instead, I needed to unravel her from within, to start small, unnoticed, like poison spreading through the veins. My thoughts turned to the children she carried, or rather, the children she claimed to carry. It was common knowledge that heirs would strengthen her standing—solidify her as queen. Without them, her claim would falter. What use was a queen who could not produce the future of the bloodline?

I moved to the window, the moon casting its silvery light over the room. Outside, the night was quiet, save for the distant rustle of the wind against the castle walls. The peace felt delicate, fragile, much like the throne she sat upon. Her barrenness would be her downfall.

If I could ensure she bore no children, or if whispers of her inability spread like wildfire, then her power would begin to erode. The dragon clans would see her as weak, unfit to sit beside Calira as his queen. With no heirs, her bloodline would wither, and with it, her influence. I would not need to lift a blade against her—not directly. The seeds of doubt would be enough to bring her low.

The plan took root in my mind, weaving itself into a quilt of deception. It was not enough to destroy her claim; I needed to sow uncertainty, slowly enough that no one would suspect my hand in her downfall. But I had time. And time was all I needed.

Turning back to Calira, who sat watching me with an intensity that left my skin tingling, I forced a calm smile. He had set this path before me, and I would follow it—just not in the way he imagined.

"There will be no need for bloodshed," I said, my voice soft but firm, the spark of ambition flickering behind my words. "We shall start with something far more subtle. Her strength lies in the children she promises to bear. If those children never come, her claim will crumble—without a war."

Calira's eyes darkened, considering my words, his hand flexing as though the idea both intrigued and unsettled him. He leaned forward, his gaze locked onto mine, and I felt the weight of his trust, the unspoken pact that now bound us together.

"Do what you must," he murmured, his voice low, reverberating through the chamber like a vow. "Make her fall without a single drop of blood being spilled. But ensure her downfall is certain."

I nodded, my mind already spinning with possibilities. The queen's reign would soon come to an end. But it would not be by sword or flame. No, her undoing would come slowly, insidiously, and by the time anyone realized what had been done, it would be far too late.

I stepped closer to him, my heart racing, not from fear but from the thrill of the power I was about to seize. The queen had held her throne long enough. Now it was my turn to rise. And I would stop at nothing to claim what was mine.

Once Calira's wounds were tightly bound and I had coaxed him to drink the bitter tonic for his pain, I helped him into the bed, his body heavy with exhaustion. His eyelids fluttered, betraying the war he fought within—between the fierce warrior who despised weakness and the wounded man who could not fight sleep any longer.

As his breathing deepened, signaling the pull of slumber, I stood over him for a moment, watching the lines of his face soften, his strength momentarily surrendered. This was the man I would fight for, the man who had placed his trust—and his heart—in my hands. But now, there was another battle ahead. One fought not with swords, but with whispers and shadows. A far more dangerous one.

Quietly, I gathered my herbs, each one carefully selected for what was to come. The earthy scent of dried roots and crushed leaves filled the chamber, mingling with the faint crackle of the fire that had long since settled into glowing embers. Tonight, the plan would begin to take shape, the first delicate roots of deception slipping into the soil of Alexandria's reign.

Her words, her command, echoed in my mind. The queen had asked me to tend to her in her chambers. She believed I would care for her, comfort her in her time of distress. But I would be planting something far more potent than comfort—something that would begin to fracture her power from within.

I moved toward the door, my fingers brushing the cool iron latch, my mind already calculating the steps ahead. I would see to

Alexandria, as she wished. But as I brewed her tea, as I mixed her herbs, I would also plant the seeds of doubt, of weakness. Subtle things at first, whispers of concern over her children, the promise of a remedy to help her bear strong heirs. But the herbs I would choose would have another purpose, one far more insidious.

If the queen could not bear the heirs she so desperately promised, her throne would crumble beneath her. Slowly, gradually, until she found herself alone, standing in the ruins of her once-great reign.

With one final glance at Calira, resting peacefully at last, I slipped from the room. The stone halls stretched ahead of me, silent and cold, but I moved with purpose, my steps measured. The night was mine, and with it, the future I had begun to carve out in the shadows.

Tonight, the seeds of my plan would be planted. And soon, they would grow into something far greater—something unstoppable. Alexandria's reign was already beginning to wither. She just didn't know it yet.

I rapped firmly on Alexandria's chamber door, my knuckles striking the wood with a purpose that belied the calm mask I wore. The weight of what I was about to set into motion coursed through me, but I kept my breath steady. Soon enough, the door creaked open, and there she stood—radiant, despite her recent tears, with a soft, kind smile on her lips. She welcomed me with a warmth that would have charmed anyone else.

"Please, come in," she said gently, stepping aside to allow me entry.

I crossed the threshold, and her chambers enveloped me like a different world altogether. The air was sweet and perfumed, heavy with the scent of roses and lavender. Everywhere I looked, there were flowers—bouquets spilling from vases, petals carefully arranged along the mantles and windowsills. It was a room of delicate beauty, an homage to the gardens she so loved. Soft linens in shades of cream and blush draped her bed, while tapestries embroidered with vines and blossoms adorned the walls. The whole space felt like an escape, a world apart from the harsh realities of court life.

But beneath the floral scent and the fragile beauty of the room, there was a vulnerability—one I intended to exploit.

"Thank you, my lady," I said, dipping my head slightly, my voice sweetened with the same warmth she had offered me. I could see the faint lines of weariness on her face, the traces of grief she had tried to hide. Her hand lingered near her abdomen for a fleeting moment, a silent reminder of the life she carried.

"You must be exhausted," I continued, my tone carefully woven with sympathy as I set down my satchel of herbs. "It is no small burden you bear, my queen."

Alexandria sighed softly, moving toward her bed, her steps slow and heavy. "It has been... difficult," she admitted, her voice barely above a whisper. "I do my best to remain strong for the realm, for Calira, but..." She trailed off, her gaze lowering to the floor.

"Of course," I replied, stepping closer, my eyes catching hers with a look of understanding. "You carry the weight of an entire kingdom, and now—" I allowed my gaze to drift ever so slightly toward her stomach, "—you carry the future as well."

Her smile faltered just slightly, and I knew I had found my opening.

"Shall I prepare something to ease your weariness?" I offered, keeping my voice gentle and inviting, my hands already reaching for the herbs I had brought. "I have just the thing to help you rest and strengthen the life within you."

Her eyes softened with gratitude, nodding as she sat on the edge of her bed, folding her hands in her lap. She trusted me, utterly and completely. And that trust would be her undoing.

As I moved to the table to prepare her tea, I selected the herbs with care—just enough to soothe her, to ease her body into rest, but mixed with something else. Something that would begin to work quietly, unnoticed. An herb known to wither life before it could ever take root. The queen would never suspect. She would continue to smile kindly, her warmth never wavering, even as the life she carried slowly faded, slipping away before anyone could realize.

I stirred the mixture, watching the steam rise from the cup. I turned back to Alexandria, offering the cup with both hands, a smile on my lips. "Drink, my queen," I said softly. "Let this bring you the peace you deserve."

She reached for the cup, her fingers brushing mine, and for a moment, I felt a pang deep within me, but it quickly dissolved. There was no room for hesitation now. What had been set in motion could not be undone.

As she lifted the cup to her lips, I watched, my heart steady, my mind already spinning ahead to the next step in my plan.

"There has been bleeding, Tonisa," Alexandria whispered, her voice trembling with the weight of the confession. She stood before me, fragile as a bloom just before it wilts. "In both my forms." Her hands moved instinctively to her abdomen, a protective gesture that now seemed hollow. "I no longer feel the hatchlings move within me. The life that once stirred... it's gone."

Her words hung heavy between us, thickening the air with sorrow and something darker—a sense of finality. My heart raced, though I kept my expression calm, neutral, careful not to betray the flicker of triumph beneath the surface. This was exactly what I had intended, but now it came to pass so quickly, almost too easily. The seed I had planted was already beginning to take root.

"I fear," she continued, her voice breaking as she blinked away tears, "that the stress of everything has damaged them." She swallowed hard, looking down at the floor as though ashamed to meet my eyes. "I just couldn't bring myself to tell Calira. Not with all that's been happening… I couldn't burden him with this."

My breath stilled, a slow pulse of satisfaction curling inside me, though I forced my face into a mask of sympathy. I took a step closer, placing a gentle hand on her arm, offering comfort I did not feel.

"Alexandria," I murmured, my voice soft, coaxing her to meet my gaze. "You've carried so much, more than any queen should have to bear alone. But you cannot keep this from him. He deserves to know." My words were laced with false compassion, every syllable carefully crafted to push her deeper into the pit of despair.

She shook her head, her breath catching in her throat as a tear slipped down her cheek. "I don't know if I can face him, not like this," she whispered, her grip tightening on the folds of her gown. "He's been so distant, so consumed by his own struggles. What if… what if this is the final blow? What if losing the hatchlings drives him away entirely?"

Her fear was evident, her desperation clinging to every word. And for a moment, I allowed her to wallow in it, to feel the full weight of her loss, of the crumbling future she had so desperately clung to. But I knew better than to let her linger too long in indecision.

"You are his queen," I said softly, my hand still resting lightly on her arm. "But even queens need help when the burdens become too great. Let me be your strength in this. Together, we can help him understand. Perhaps... perhaps there's still hope."

Her eyes searched mine, seeking reassurance, but what she found was carefully veiled calculation. She nodded slowly, her spirit too weary to fight against the comfort I offered.

"Perhaps," she echoed, though her voice was faint, the conviction behind it long gone.

I watched her closely, each second that passed bringing her closer to the inevitable truth. The queen was breaking. And with her, the fragile peace she had held together would soon unravel. But it wasn't enough yet. She had to fall completely, her claim shattered beyond repair. Only then could I stand beside Calira, not as a mere servant or confidante, but as the queen this realm truly needed.

For now, I had to play the part of the loyal supporter, a shoulder for Alexandria to lean on as her world slowly collapsed.

"Rest now," I urged, guiding her toward her bed, my tone soft and soothing. "You've done all you can. Let me take care of everything else. I'll speak with Calira when the time is right. For now, focus on yourself, on healing. Perhaps the gods still have a plan for you."

She lay back on her bed, exhaustion weighing her down, her hope hanging by a thread. As I moved to leave, a smile threatened to tug at the corners of my lips. But I hid it well.

"Tonisa," Alexandria said softly, her voice heavy with resignation. "At first light, when both my husband and I have had time to rest, please bring him to my chambers—alone. I will take your counsel and share with him my fears regarding our children." Her gaze flickered with uncertainty, her resolve fragile, but I could see the quiet determination that had finally taken root.

"Of course, my queen," I replied with a bow of my head, my voice as smooth and reassuring as ever. "I shall ensure he is brought to your chambers at dawn and that no one disturbs your moment of privacy. You both deserve to speak without interruption, and I will see to it that your wishes are honored."

I met her gaze, holding it for just a moment longer, offering her the comfort of certainty. Inside, the wheels of my plan turned with silent precision, each piece falling perfectly into place.

TWENTY- ONE

The day had finally arrived—the day Calira would face his wife, and I would step closer to claiming my destiny. The weight of it settled over me like a shroud, but beneath the calm exterior, anticipation thrummed through my veins.

At first light, I went to him, gently waking him from his slumber. His eyes fluttered open, still heavy with the remnants of sleep, but there was more strength in his gaze than the days prior. The tinctures and herbs I had used had done their work, and though his wounds still marred his skin, his spirit had returned.

"Good morning, my lord," I murmured as I helped him rise, his muscles stiff but no longer weakened by pain.

I guided him to the basin, where warm water steamed gently, and set about washing him with care. His skin, though bruised and scarred, was smooth beneath my touch, and the exhaustion that had weighed him down had begun to lift. The firelight flickered across the room, casting long shadows as I worked, tending to him as I always had—yet knowing this day, everything would change.

Once bathed and refreshed, I made sure he was fed, the simple meal sustaining him without overwhelming his healing body. He ate in silence, the tension in the air tangible as both of us prepared for what was to come. His gaze flickered to mine occasionally, as though he could sense something shifting between us, though he said nothing.

Afterward, I dressed him in the finest dark tunic, the rich fabric complementing the stygian black of his long hair. With deft hands, I braided the silken strands, weaving them with precision. The familiarity of the task was comforting, a reminder of all the moments we had shared, but today the braid felt like more than a symbol of care—it felt like preparation for battle.

As my fingers worked through his hair, I allowed myself a moment to savor the closeness, the unspoken bond between us. His strength had returned, his wounds no longer the frail, festering things they had been when he first returned to me. He was more himself now, the man who had captured my heart—and my future.

When I finished, I stepped back, allowing my eyes to take in the man before me. He looked every bit the warrior, tall and proud, though the shadows of the past days lingered in the edges of his expression. His wounds were mended, but the confrontation that lay ahead weighed heavily on both of us.

"Are you ready, my lord?" I asked softly, searching his face.

He nodded, the resolve in his eyes unmistakable. "I am."

I offered him a faint smile and moved to his side, placing my hand lightly on his arm. The hour had come for Calira to face his wife—and for me to take the next step in my plan.

We made our way down the dim corridor to Alexandria's chambers, the weight of the moment heavy between us. The door, surprisingly, was slightly ajar, the sliver of space revealing only shadow beyond. A cold unease settled in my chest, but before I could speak, Calira pushed the door open fully and stepped inside.

The moment he crossed the threshold, his sharp intake of breath filled the room.

"Alexandria!" he cried, rushing forward.

I followed close behind, and the scene that awaited us was more horrific than anything I could have imagined. Alexandria sat slumped in a chair, her once regal form crumpled and broken, blood staining the delicate fabric of her gown. Her face was streaked with tears, her eyes hollow with grief, but it was not her that drew Calira's gasp.

At her feet, three small dragon hatchlings lay lifeless, their once-glimmering scales dulled, their tiny bodies drenched in a pool of blood that spread out in crimson arcs across the floor. They were still, unnaturally so, their fragile forms twisted in death.

The queen's sobs tore through the silence, raw and anguished, as she clung to Calira, burying her face in his chest. His arms instinctively wrapped around her, holding her tightly, though the shock in his eyes betrayed the devastation that had pierced his soul.

I remained frozen for a moment, the enormity of what had happened settling over me like a dark shroud. The hatchlings— the heirs that would have secured Alexandria's claim, the very lives I had sought to prevent—now lay dead before her. But not like this. Not so suddenly. It was as though fate itself had reached out and twisted my intentions, the outcome far more brutal than even I had planned.

I took a slow step forward, intending to offer some semblance of comfort, to help in whatever way I could. But before I could draw closer, Alexandria's tear-filled eyes snapped up, her gaze filled with raw fury and sorrow. She raised a trembling hand, signaling me to stop.

"Stay back!" she cried, her voice breaking as she clutched at Calira. "Leave us… please, leave us."

The grief in her voice was so deep it struck like a physical blow. I hesitated, caught between my instincts to act and the unspoken knowledge that nothing I could say or do would ease her suffering. My hands trembled at my sides, the weight of what had transpired pressing against me.

I took a step back, my heart racing, and watched as the king cradled his broken queen. Her weeping filled the chamber, raw and unrelenting, and for the first time, I realized that this was no mere game of power. The cost of ambition, the weight of fate's cruelty, was far heavier than I had anticipated.

I retreated quietly, my presence no longer welcome in the sea of their grief. The queen had lost more than her children that day—she had lost everything. And as I stood in the shadows, I wondered how much more would be lost before this all came to an end.

I closed the door softly behind me, pressing my ear to the wood in the hope of catching their whispered words. But instead, there was nothing—nothing but the sound of Alexandria's heart-wrenching weeping, a deep, unrelenting sob that echoed through the stillness of the hall. My heart raced as I strained to hear more, but no discussion came, no plans or accusations passed between them. Only grief.

A moment later, the door creaked open, and Calira stepped out, his expression carved from stone. In his arms, he cradled the three lifeless hatchlings, their small bodies wrapped delicately in the bloodstained linens that had once covered the royal bed. His movements were slow, deliberate, as though the weight of what he carried was more than he could bear.

As the door closed behind him with a soft thud, a piercing wail erupted from within—Alexandria's voice, raw and anguished, carrying through the castle like the mourning cry of a broken soul. The walls seemed to tremble with it, the very air heavy with sorrow.

Calira turned the key in the lock, sealing her inside, as though even that small action might offer some control in a world spiraling into chaos. His eyes, dark and sharp, locked onto mine, searching for something I wasn't sure I could give. His jaw clenched as he adjusted the weight of the bloodied bundle in one arm, his free hand reaching for me, pulling me forward with a strength that left no room for hesitation.

"Was this your doing, Tonisa?" he asked, his voice low but filled with something dangerous, like a blade unsheathed.

I met his gaze, the accusation clear in his tone but tempered by the confusion and pain that swirled within him. My heart pounded, but I held my composure, knowing full well that the slightest misstep now could ruin everything.

"No," I replied calmly, my voice steady as I forced myself to remain collected. "The tea I gave her would not have worked so swiftly. What has happened here is the will of the gods, nothing more."

His grip on my arm tightened, his eyes narrowing as though searching my face for any hint of deception.

"Though," I added, allowing a small, careful smile to touch my lips, "I will admit... the gods seem to have aligned in my favor."

His eyes darkened further, a storm brewing behind them. He said nothing, but the tension between us was a thick, invisible thread that seemed to tighten with every passing moment. There was an unspoken truth now, a shift in the air between us. The queen's children were gone, her claim weakened, and fate, it seemed, had begun to tilt in my direction.

But whether Calira saw this as divine intervention or something far more sinister, I could not tell. He remained silent, his gaze hard and unreadable as he continued down the corridor, pulling me along in his wake. And as we moved away from the locked chamber and the queen's cries, I felt the weight of his question still hanging between us.

For now, the gods—or fate, or whatever power had intervened—had set the stage for my rise. But I knew that Calira, and the realm itself, would demand answers. And when that moment came, I would be ready.

"I am not angry with you, Tonisa," Calira murmured, his voice soft but weighted with exhaustion. His grip on my arm loosened, and his tone shifted, the edge of suspicion replaced by something far more vulnerable. "It is all just happening so fast, my love. I…"

He trailed off, his words drifting into the silence as he stopped before the tall, arched window. His gaze fixed on the horizon, his face suddenly shadowed with an emotion I could not yet name. I followed his line of sight, my breath catching as I saw what had drawn his attention—far in the distance, miles away, the banners of Crystal Springs flew high and proud, their vivid colors unmistakable against the dull gray sky.

His father had returned.

Ramsra's army was visible even from here, the shimmering lines of soldiers, their armor gleaming in the morning light, stretching across the valley. It was a sight both awe-inspiring and foreboding, a reminder that the peace we had clung to was fragile at best.

"It would seem," Calira said quietly, his voice rough with a mixture of resignation and acceptance, "that I am king no longer, my beloved. Now, the true test begins."

He turned back to me then, his face still etched with the weight of the moment, but something else flickered in his eyes—something fierce, something determined. His free hand, the one not cradling the tragic remains of the hatchlings, reached for me. Before I could speak, before I could offer him any words of comfort, his lips crashed against mine.

The kiss was raw, intense, filled with both passion and desperation. His fingers tangled into my hair, his fist tightening as though he feared letting go would mean losing me to the chaos that had begun to swirl around us. I melted into him, feeling the heat of his body, the way he pulled me closer, his kiss a promise that, no matter the storm on the horizon, he would fight for us.

His breath mingled with mine, rough and heavy, the force of his kiss igniting a fire within me, one that mirrored the flames of ambition and desire already burning deep inside. This was the man I had always known—the warrior, the king. And though he no longer wore the crown, his power was undeniable.

When he finally pulled away, his forehead pressed gently to mine, his breathing ragged, he whispered, "Whatever comes next, I will not face it alone."

The truth of his words wrapped around us like a vow. And as I looked into his eyes, fierce and filled with passion, I knew that the games of the court had only just begun. Ramsra's return would challenge everything—his rule, our plans, and my place at his side. But as the storm gathered outside, I was ready to weather it. I had played my part in setting this course, and now, with Calira bound to me in more ways than one, I would fight to see it through. The future hung in the balance, but together, we would shape it to our will.